The Forgotten Land

A hardened frontiersman, known only as Bannock, and his friend Chet Butler are escorting members of a religious sect, the Children of God, through the wastes of Sonora in northern Mexico. The colonists, eager to be free from persecution, have fled the USA in search of a new home. Unfortunately for the strict pacifists, a band of raiding Comanches finds them first. Following a desperate battle, Bannock flees for his life through the desert. After a tortuous journey he stumbles, more dead than alive, upon an old Spanish mission, long abandoned by its priests. In their place is a small settlement of poorly armed peons, barely scraping a living, and in permanent fear of Indian marauders. Building a bond with his saviours, Bannock reluctantly decides that he is all done with running, and that whatever terrors the 'Comanche Moon' brings, they will face them together!

The Forgotten Land

Paul Bedford

A Black Horse Western

ROBERT HALE

© Paul Bedford 2018
First published in Great Britain 2018

ISBN 978-0-7198-2773-0

The Crowood Press
The Stable Block
Crowood Lane
Ramsbury
Marlborough
Wiltshire SN8 2HR

www.bhwesterns.com

Robert Hale is an imprint
of The Crowood Press

Typeset by
Derek Doyle & Associates, Shaw Heath
Printed and bound in Great Britain by
4Bind Ltd, Stevenage, SG1 2XT

Author's Note

This book is based on a short story that I wrote at the tender age of seventeen, which unbelievably is now forty-five years ago. How time flies!

CHAPTER ONE

The man known only as Bannock stared out over the desolate terrain and sighed deeply. Every move that he made seemed to extract more sweat from his weary body, and yet he knew there would be no relief until the sun went down. Under the meagre shade of his hat brim, hard eyes that were never still unremittingly scanned his surroundings. He had discovered long before that out on the frontier even a moment's inattention could be more than enough to get him killed, and so he had adopted the mountain man's survival routine of habitual watchfulness.

As his horse whinnied beneath him, he muttered, 'Yeah, yeah, so we're both thirsty.'

In truth, he couldn't remember a time when he hadn't been. The relentless, searing heat seemed to be grilling his innards. Only unforgiving and apparently endless desert lay before him – and yet unbelievably this was what his charges had come in search of. Their stated objective was isolation from anything human, and by God they'd certainly achieved that.

Sonora, in the Year of Our Lord 1843, was sparsely populated by anyone's reckoning. Spanish missionaries had formerly ventured into this land, but some of their savage parishioners had proven too much even for their dogged persistence. With Mexico City far, far away to the south, the region suffered under the maxim 'out of sight, out of mind'. Beset by the depredations of various wild tribes, and yet insufficiently profitable to justify the expense of military protection, it had effectively been left to its own devices. And yet there was always someone prepared to take a chance on land forsaken by others.

Leather creaked slightly, as Bannock shifted his weight in the well-worn saddle. The sound of shod hoofs had reached his ears, and he knew without turning that it could only be his companion coming to join him. Perversely, it was at that very moment that the one thing he had dreaded above all else came to his attention. About to toss a casual insult in the other man's direction, he was abruptly distracted by movement on the horizon. A great deal of movement!

A large band of horsemen had swept into view, and as the dust settled around them, they casually sat their animals, scrutinizing him as a spider might a fly caught in its web. Despite the gruelling temperature, a chill abruptly enveloped his lean body, accompanied by an involuntary tremor that could only have been generated by past experience. For only one tribe possessed the arrogance to ride so blatantly through open country, as though they had nothing to fear from anyone. Had he been an imaginative individual, he might have wished for the ground to swallow him up, but Bannock had long before ceased to take account of anything other than harsh realities.

Turning his head slightly, he asked of his friend, 'You see 'em?'

'I see 'em.'

'What do you reckon?'

'Just looking us over . . . for now.'

'That's what I figured.'

For a long moment the two men sat their horses and, controlling their very real alarm, watched the distant figures. Both knew better than to overtly display any fear when confronting members of the savage tribes. Yet the 'Anglos' couldn't remain there forever, and finally Bannock turned to scrutinize his companion. Chet Butler didn't look anything like the archetypal spare, rangy frontiersman. Naturally muscular, he was built like a house side, and a darned big one at that. His features appeared to have been hewn out of granite, and yet he displayed laughter lines that hinted at a softer side. Sadly, there was nothing even vaguely amusing about the sight before them.

'Apaches or Yaqui, maybe?' he queried.

Bannock emphatically shook his head. 'There's only one native peoples that really chill me to the bone.'

'Comanches!' Butler exclaimed. 'This far west?'

His companion nodded grimly. 'Why not? They've travelled plenty further than this on their murder raids. Think about it. Along the Comanche Trace, out of Comancheria. Then across the Rio Grande, and through Santa Elena Canyon into Mexico. Piece of pie to them.' He spat in the dust expressively, before adding, 'As you well know. Anyhu, I've had my fill of this eyeballing shit. We hired on as guides, so let's give some guidance.' With that, he gently tugged on the reins and wheeled his mount about.

Together, yet apart, they retraced their steps. There was absolutely no point in attempting to hide their trail. The Indians who were undoubtedly following them would be able to do so over just about any terrain. *And* it was highly likely that they already knew about the wagon train.

The extended column of wagons moved slowly, wallowing in its own dust like an ageing reptile. Drawn by long teams of mules, the heavy conveyances relentlessly creaked and rattled their way on a southwesterly heading. The frequently obstinate beasts had been chosen at Bannock's insistent suggestion. Although not as large and strong as oxen, they were much more resilient in harsh conditions. With every stone and rut a major obstacle, the overlanders trudging alongside had instructions to remove any rocks from the path – though recently more often than not they just ignored them. Exhaustion had a way of sapping the spirit.

To reduce the weight on board, men, women and all but the youngest children had long accepted the need to walk, but after hundreds of miles that had taken its toll. Footwear had worn thin, and in some cases was pitiably non-existent. Their overall appearance was unremarkable, similar to any other settlers making the long, dangerous journey to a new home . . . with one startling exception. There was a complete visible absence of firearms. Instead of long rifles, the men carried stout wooden staves with which to beat or fend off snakes and other troublesome critters. Apparently unwilling or unable to hunt for food, they had brought with them a dwindling herd of cattle, to be slaughtered when fresh meat was required to enhance the monotonous diet.

With *nearly* everyone on foot, the arrival of their leader on horseback always created a slight frisson of excitement, a fact of which he was not unaware. Joshua Wilson was a big, rawboned individual, whose deep-set eyes burned with a strange and often times disturbing intensity. It was he who had instigated the long trek west, although few amongst the men folk would disagree that it had been necessary. For the 'Children of God' had suffered persecution in every part of the United States they had attempted to establish themselves. Even Texas, currently an independent republic, had displayed little inclination to accommodate them. And so, after a great deal of soul-searching, the 'Children' had taken the momentous decision to try their hand in Northern Mexico. In past times, the Mexicans had been known to welcome settlers from the north, but more important was the fact that these latest arrivals were seeking land that no others had a use for. That way they stood a chance of being left in peace.

'Move those rocks, my friends,' Wilson instructed loudly. 'Do not slacken from your task. We are all weary, but that's no excuse for a broken axle.'

A male voice called out from the far side of the lead

wagon. It was the accepted rule that all the men kept to the right of the wagons, and the women to the left, to preserve their modesty when attending to a call of nature. 'The gentiles are returning, Joshua.'

Wilson nodded. 'Happen they'll have news of a waterhole, where we can make camp for the night.' He had no great liking for the two often-times profane guides, but he had to admit that so far on the journey they had proved indispensable.

'If you ask me, God's lost interest in this crew,' Butler remarked sagely, as they approached the slow-moving wagon train.

'I didn't,' Bannock retorted.

'This sure has to be the quietest party I've ever escorted,' the other man persisted. 'No cussing of any sort, an' nobody shooting snakes. It just don't seem natural. I recall that last wagon train I took along the Platte River Road. Every minute of every God-damn day they were taking pot shots at some reptile or other. And there was always some silly bastard who managed to blow off his big toe.'

His friend grunted. 'Well, if they don't do exactly as we say tonight, they'll be as quiet as the grave come morning.'

As the two men reined in before the leader of the sect, Bannock fastened his gaze meaningfully on the other man. He had a lot to impart, but it was Wilson who got in first. 'Do I take it that you have located fresh water?' he inquired somewhat ponderously.

'No, you don't,' Bannock retorted. 'What we did find

was a shitload of trouble, and it's headed your way.'

The other man's bushy eyebrows rose imperiously. Not for the first time, he had obviously taken exception to either the tone or content of his guide's report . . . or quite possibly both. On this occasion, however, he wasn't given the chance to comment.

'We've been discovered by the orneriest creatures on God's creation. And I reckon they'll be down your throat well before first light.'

Bannock's unmistakable gravity gave the religious leader certain pause for thought. Unconsciously glancing around, he asked, 'Who are they, and what are their intentions?'

Chet Butler couldn't contain himself. 'They're most likely Pehnahterkuh Comanches from around the Edwards Plateau in Texas. Their certain intentions are to kill, rape, loot, burn and torture. They'll also carry off any of your women and children that they take a fancy to. Believe me, mister, you ain't seen *anything* like them before!'

Wilson shook his head in disbelief, before turning to the other guide. 'Mister Bannock, I hired you two *gentlemen* to lead us to the Promised Land, not bring back fanciful tales with which to frighten our children. Do you honestly expect me to believe any of what your companion here has just told me?'

That man snorted incredulously, but Bannock was quick to defend him. 'Oh, you'd better believe him, *Mister* Wilson. Because if you don't, having your hair lifted really will be the least of your worries.' That last was uttered with such sincerity that only a simpleton could have dismissed it, and whatever else he was, the sect leader was not that.

Wilson peered at his guide with a certain amount of apprehension. It finally appeared as though the gravity of the situation was sinking in. 'If there is danger such as you say, what do you propose that we do about it?'

Bannock drew in a deep breath. He finally seemed to be making some headway. 'First off, you circle the wagons. Here and now. Fresh water will have to wait. Pack them tight, nose to tail, with all your animals inside the circle, so they can't be run off. Next, get some pitch torches into the ground at intervals around the perimeter, so come nightfall the devils will know that we're ready for them. Then throw away those silly sticks you've been toting, and break out every rifle and shotgun you possess.'

The other man gazed at him in astonishment. 'There are *no* firearms of any description in any of the wagons. I told you that when we first set out. We abhor violence of any kind.'

Butler laughed out loud. 'We thought you was just funning with us, mister. What sort of lame-brained fool would cross this land without having a gun or three to hand?'

His companion fiercely massaged his temple, as though trying to make sense of what he had just heard. It was only with difficulty that Bannock kept his voice calm and level. 'Whatever your beliefs, there's no gain-saying that trouble has caught up with you,' he unrelentingly announced. 'So you're gonna have to turn mean. Real mean. Chet and I are packing quite a

14

lot of shooting irons. If you people work with us, we might *just* be able to bluff those heathen sons of bitches into thinking this wagon train's too much to handle.'

Wilson shook his head emphatically. The fact that all the wagons had halted, and many of his people were listening to Bannock's dire prophecies, didn't seem to faze him in the slightest. 'I appreciate your concern, my friend, but you really don't seem to comprehend what we stand for at all. We are totally committed to non-violence. That is why we have come all the way out here, away from the rowdy aggression and intolerance of the United States. These Comanches that you talk of are surely just simple peoples, afraid for their own safety. They believe that we mean them harm. If I greet them with open arms, and assure them of our peaceful intentions, I have no doubt that they will leave us be.'

As Butler uttered a hoot of derision and turned away, Bannock glanced around at the gathering settlers. 'Now you pilgrims listen to me, and listen good. Your leader may be well intentioned, but he has no idea of what you're up against. I do. Trust me, when I say that the only way for you to survive this night is to work with us and fight back.'

A sea of dusty, sweat-stained faces absorbed his words, but not one man reacted as he had hoped. Most just shook their heads in bewilderment. Then, quite bizarrely considering the circumstances, they appeared to simply lose interest and turned their attention to other tasks.

With frustration turning to raw anger, the frontiersman's eyes suddenly settled on a particularly appealing young girl standing next to the lead wagon. Natural curls were enhanced by the delightful red bonnet protecting her from the sun's rays, and her adorable features wore a look of innocence that could only be fleeting in such a harsh world. Seizing on her likely fate, he abruptly advanced on a startled Joshua Wilson. Flecks of spittle flew from Bannock's mouth, as he unleashed a tirade.

'You see her?' he demanded. 'If she doesn't die in the first rush, she'll like as not get carried off by some Comanche buck. He'll treat her worse than a dog, and let the old women burn holes in her flesh just for the hell of it. And then, and only if she's really lucky, she might get adopted by the tribe, but more likely they'll sell her off to some band of Comancheros from New Mexico. Either way, she'll very quickly be unrecognizable as a white girl, and all because *you* ain't got the guts to fight back.' Even as he spoke, Bannock was aware of tears welling up in the girl's eyes, but there could be no help for it. He was doing his damnedest to provoke the sect leader.

That individual was indeed getting angry, but sadly not enough and not for the right reasons. Wiping Bannock's saliva from his face, he admonished, 'You are frightening the girl for no good reason. I will thank you to cease immediately and leave us. You are no longer welcome in our company.'

The other man clenched his right fist, as though about to strike. 'Well, that just about cuts it. You really are one stupid, ornery son of a bitch. What is it that gives you the right to risk their lives like this?'

A strange serenity appeared on Wilson's face, as he half turned towards his 'flock' and spread his arms in apparent supplication. '*They* have given me the right.'

Bannock's scorn turned to resignation, as he abruptly realized that there was simply no getting through to such a fanatic. Without another word, he turned on his heels and rejoined his companion. Together they moved off until out of earshot of the 'Children of God'.

'I don't recall you ever stringing that many words together before,' Butler slyly remarked. 'Just remind me why we took on this job in the first place.'

'You know damn well why,' his friend replied. 'Because their silver dollars are as good as anybody else's. That said, I reckon our contract has just come to an abrupt end.'

'So what's next?' the big man enquired.

Bannock shrugged. 'Since we can't do nothing for them, all we can do is save ourselves.'

'And how do you propose we do that? I don't reckon running's an option, 'cause those bastards'll surely have us surrounded by now.'

'I know. That's why we're going to start digging instead.'

Butler gawped in amazement. 'Dig what? Our own graves?'

'Huh, that'll be the day,' Bannock grunted. 'No, we're gonna fort up. You see that small rise over yonder? Well, just in front of it, we'll dig a trench big enough for the two of us to crouch in, and pile the earth up in front. That way, when the Comanches

17

sweep in to attack the wagon train, they won't see us . . . hopefully.'

'What about the horses?'

The other man grimaced. 'Ah, well, that's the rub. They *will* be spotted, so we'll just have to leave them with the pilgrims.'

Butler was aghast. 'You'd set us afoot in the desert?'

'Either that, or get butchered for sure! Which'll it be?'

CHAPTER TWO

Darkness, such as it was, had fallen long before, almost unnoticed by the sweating men. Sadly, under the circumstances, a near perfect 'Comanche moon' bathed the landscape in an eerie glow, which *should* have unsettled any perceptive individual travelling in Indian country. The dugout was finished, tin plates having doubled as entrenching tools. Now all that remained was for them to check over their weapons.

Glancing over at the wagons, some fifty yards away, Butler shook his head for maybe the tenth time that night. 'God-damned stupid sons of bitches,' he muttered scathingly. The trail-worn conveyances had been circled, but apparently with the sole intention of preventing their owners' animals from wandering off. There were no flaming torches in evidence, and almost unbelievably not one single sentry.

'I've got to admit, it's almost like they have some kind of death wish,' Bannock quietly concurred. 'And what really breaks me up, is what's likely to happen to that little girl with the red bonnet. Did you see her? She

19

was just the cutest creature, and yet she's got no say in anything.'

'Best not to think on it,' his huge companion replied. 'It'll just take your mind off of what needs to be done, and sure as hell won't change the outcome.'

'I guess you've got the right of it,' Bannock very reluctantly accepted, as he set to examining his brace of Paterson Colts.

As the frontiersman had earlier stated, the two men were indeed 'packing' a lot of iron. In addition to his modern five-shot revolvers, Bannock possessed a hand-made .50 calibre muzzle-loading Hawken rifle, which boasted double-set triggers and 'honest' sights. A large hunting knife in the 'Bowie' style completed his armoury. By contrast, Chet Butler favoured a pair of rather dated, single-shot percussion pistols and, bizarrely, an absolutely immense Nock volleygun. Most men would have considered this antique piece, with its dated flintlock mechanism, to be a dangerous and unwieldy curiosity. With six 20in barrels grouped around a seventh, it unleashed, more or less simultaneously, a volley that could be devastating against close-packed assailants. However, its many drawbacks included a massively heavyweight, bone-crushing recoil, and the time it took to reload the barrels individually. Butler, who had purchased it from an English naval deserter many years earlier, treasured it as an effective, if somewhat temperamental man killer, and wouldn't hear anything said against it. Certainly only someone of his great size and strength could have controlled such a weapon.

'Seems like we're as ready as we're ever gonna be,' Bannock remarked in hushed tones. 'I reckon we'll take it in turns to get a little shuteye.'

Other than the occasional movement of the enclosed animals, all was silent over by the circled wagons. The surrounding landscape appeared empty, just as on any previous night, but that didn't fool the two guides. The Comanches were out there for sure, and would undoubtedly make a lethal appearance at a time of their own choosing. Both men had a pretty fair idea of what to expect, but if they were afraid they made a good job of concealing the fact. They knew full well that if fear got the upper hand, then they were as good as dead already.

Recognizing that when the attack came, there would likely be no time for any sentiment, Bannock took his friend's hand in a firm grip. 'Just make sure that damned cannon's nowhere near me, if and when you get to trigger it,' he instructed with a warm smile.

'Don't go troubling yourself,' Butler retorted softly, as he returned the pressure. 'To my certain knowledge, I've never yet kilt a friend with it.'

'Well, ain't that just reassuring?' Bannock drolly commented. With that, the two men settled down to pass what remained of the calm before the storm. Neither of them was under any illusions as to what lay ahead, but at least they were 'loaded for bear', as the frontier parlance went!

The war party was large, amounting to well in excess of one hundred copper-toned warriors, and they could almost taste the glorious victory that would surely be theirs. Normally Comanches were wary of attacking large groups of well armed settlers, but their scouts had been tracking this party for a couple of days, and two factors now emboldened them to strike. Firstly, the travellers appeared to have come from Texas, and the horse Indians of the southern plains hated *Tejanos* easily as much as they did Mexicans. Secondly, and quite remarkably, other than the two guides, they seemed to be armed solely with wooden sticks. At first that discovery had filled them with alarm. To a people ruled by omens and signs, such behaviour indicated that the white men had no fear of anyone that they might encounter, and thus possessed great power. But then their war chief, Set-tainte, had berated his men as never before. These wagon people were merely simple crop-tenders, not the much-feared rangers who had fought the Comanches so fiercely in West Texas.

And so it was decided. Shortly before dawn, the war party split into two groups. The smallest, numbering only twenty men, was charged with running off all the animals to the safety of a box canyon some short distance away. The rest were to attack the wagons. Designated members of that latter band carried flaming brushwood, with which to burn out the settlers. With practised speed, the savage horde swept towards the remarkably silent circle, their path illuminated by silvery moonlight. Unbelievably there appeared to be no sentries to warn of their approach.

Traditionally, none of the sinewy warriors would even countenance fighting on foot, so they attached rawhide ropes to one of the wagons whilst still mounted, and then urged their ponies to take the strain. As a gap opened up, two things happened. Those tasked with stealing the livestock surged into the inner circle, and the helpless occupants of the wagon awoke to face a living nightmare.

A bewildered young woman peered out through the canvas flaps, and stared in sheer horror at the barely clothed savages before her. The scream beginning to form in the base of her throat turned into a muted death rattle, as a barbed arrow slammed into her body. Emboldened at having drawn first blood, the Comanches unleashed great whoops of joy, and began to drive the settlers' terrified animals over towards the widening gap. They were confident in the knowledge that even then their comrades were attacking the wagons from outside of the circle.

It was only as the sun-baked canopies above their heads began to ignite, that a sickening realization struck the 'Children of God' with razor-sharp clarity. Chet Butler's graphic description of their likely fate was coming true. As they leapt clear of their burning 'homes', howling fiends rode at them from every direction. A Comanche warrior was only truly in his element when mounted. It was as though pony and rider were one, and with their prey out in the open, there could be no stopping the slaughter.

Joshua Wilson watched in dismay as all their assorted animals were driven off into the night – but that was just the prelude. Because then the screaming started, and not just by women and children. As the sect leader

23

clambered down from his wagon, one of the men of his 'flock' stumbled past, seemingly out of his mind with pain. Unbelievably, the hair on his head had apparently been completely sliced off, leaving a raw scalp covered in blood. Mounted savages were riding back and forth with complete impunity, expertly weaving around their victims. Razor-sharp lances skewered running men, as though for sport, whilst others were struck down by deftly aimed arrows.

Wide-eyed with shock, Wilson rushed into the midst of the killing ground, his head and arms raised to the heavens. 'For pity's sake, stop!' he implored. 'There is no need for this.'

The Comanches who witnessed this display regarded him with a mixture of suspicion and amusement. Unsure as to where his entreaties were directed, they understood not a single word that he had uttered, and even if they had it would have made no difference. They had no pity for their enemies, and there was every need to continue the butchery, because brutal warfare was in their blood. And yet, for a moment, they held off from slaughtering the strange white man. Primitive superstition had provided him with a temporary reprieve.

With the full horror backlit by the burning wagons, some of the menfolk desperately fought back with any-thing that came to hand. Whips, knives and their pathetic wooden staves were all pressed into service – but it was all too little, too late. As more and more set-tlers succumbed in a welter of blood, the Indians turned their attention to the women and children.

The young girl who had so captivated Bannock, peered out from under the wagon bed. Frantically she searched for any sign of her parents. Then, illuminated by the soaring flames, she spotted her mother being forced to the ground by one of their terrifying attackers. Despite her hysterical screams, the frenzied apparition was tearing at her clothing. The reason for this peculiar behaviour eluded her, and yet instinct told her she had to help. Tightly clutching the red bonnet that was her pride and joy, the little figure raced from cover . . . straight into the path of a fast-moving pony.

With incredible dexterity, the warrior simultaneously manoeuvred his mount aside and swept her off her feet. In the firm grip of a bronzed fiend, all the youngster could do was emulate her mother and scream . . . and scream.

For Joshua Wilson, still miraculously untouched by the bloody carnage, this new development was just too much to endure, even for a sworn pacifist. Unexpectedly overcome by a murderous rage, he charged to the child's aid. Although a stranger to violence, his large frame nevertheless held great power. Coming up behind the abductor, Wilson seized hold of the Comanche's waist and dragged him from his pony. Taken by surprise, that man released his captive and snatched a hunting knife from his breechclout.

Seeing the deadly threat, Wilson abruptly changed his grip. Wrapping his left arm around the Indian's neck, he grabbed the head with his right and heaved with all his might. Although the sound of a bone snapping was inaudible over the noisy chaos, for some reason the lone white man, still incandescent with rage, momentarily attracted a great deal of attention. As all resistance abruptly ceased, he released his victim like so much rubbish, and bawled out his defiance at the startled Indians closest to him.

'Leave us be, you murdering sons of Satan, or the power of the Lord will surely smite you all!'

Temporarily ignored, the little girl continued the determined dash towards her mother. That poor woman, flat on the ground and with her clothes torn to pieces, was desperately trying to fend off the fierce advances of her captor. As her distraught daughter suddenly appeared before her, the anguished mother caught a brief glimpse through tear-stained eyes and cried out, 'Run, my sweet baby. Run while you can!'

With almost casual disdain, the lustful Comanche buck turned and delivered a stinging backhand slap that knocked the troublesome child off her feet. Then, as behind him a dozen warriors surrounded Joshua Wilson, he commenced a vicious sexual assault on the woman beneath him.

Even as the sect leader recognized that his time had come, he also realized that the two guides had been right all along, and that there were indeed times when only violence could answer. And so, as the unforgiving figures around him notched their arrows, he turned to the full moon and howled out, 'Avenge us, Bannock!' Those were the last words he uttered on God's earth, because at that moment a flight of barbed shafts pierced his chest, snuffing out his life with graphic finality.

If his plea had been heard, there was no response. The Comanches continued with their accustomed rape and slaughter. The leisurely torture of captives would wait until they were far away, and safe from any possible pursuit. Struggling to hold back her tears, the little girl got to her feet and stared uncomprehendingly at her mother's terrible ordeal. She had absolutely no idea what to do, but suddenly the decision was made for her. From out of nowhere another mounted warrior surged towards her and quite literally swept her off her feet. Remarkably, she still clutched her treasured possession, the little red bonnet.

Chet Butler stared in abject horror as he observed his companion level his Hawken rifle. 'Just what the hell are you fixing to do with that?' he quietly demanded. Strangely, under the changing circumstances, he was still concerned with keeping quiet to avoid detection.

The sharpshooter grimly drew a bead on the diminutive target. 'There's only one thing I can do to save that adorable child from a fate worse than death itself.'

'And where will that leave *us*?' Butler asked angrily, as he quickly glanced around their position. The two men were crouching behind the pile of earth that they had excavated, their lair so far undiscovered. In deep shadow, well away from the massacre site, it was entirely possible that they would remain that way.

'Up shit creek, as usual,' Bannock retorted. 'But there really isn't any option, is there?'

Butler sighed deeply. He was probably the only person still living who had learned a little of his very private friend's past. Long ago there had been some family member whom he had not been able to save, and the memory of that had haunted him ever since. 'Knowing you as I do, I guess not,' the big man finally responded.

'You wouldn't have it any other way, anyhu,' Bannock replied. 'Fighting's in your blood.' Then he held his breath and fired.

As the heavy ball struck, blood splashed over the face of the exultant Comanche and the red bonnet fluttered down to the hard-packed earth. With surprise turning to anger, the warrior discarded his lifeless captive and emitted a tremendous war whoop. Shocked by the single unexpected gunshot, his comrades abruptly ceased their savage activities and went in search of the source. As fleet-footed ponies surged around the wagon circle, it could only be a matter of moments before the two white men were discovered.

'Now that's what I call real active,' Butler muttered laconically, as he hefted his volleygun into position.

'One of these days that cannon'll blow up in your face,' his friend remarked with a sad smile, as he swiftly reloaded the Hawken.

The massive frontiersman matched the expression. 'Let's just get past today, huh?'

Then a collective shriek emanated from the war party and the two men knew that their time had come. And yet, strangely, nothing happened immediately. With their night vision affected by the flames, the Comanches milled around in confusion, unsure as to exactly how many enemies awaited them in the makeshift redoubt. Then their leader, Set-tainte, thrust himself to the fore. Under his fierce exhortations, the assembled warriors dug in their heels and charged forwards.

Unlike his first, carefully placed shot, Bannock now had no need for the finer points of marksmanship. With scores of horsemen approaching, he merely aimed low and squeezed hard on the front trigger. There was a satisfying crash, as his shoulder absorbed the heavy recoil. The .50 calibre ball brought a pony tumbling down, which in turn tripped others following behind. Some strange sixth sense told him to hold off using his Colts, and so he grabbed his powder flask and began to recharge the Hawken.

As the Comanches drew closer, they saw that there were only two 'white eyes' opposing them. With no conception of what awaited them, they assumed that it would surely be only a matter of moments before they could return to the delights of rape and pillage.

Chet Butler hugged the stock of his big gun tightly into his right shoulder. He knew from experience that he could cope with the massive recoil . . . just. As the pounding hoofs reached the thirty-yard mark, thereby still ensuring a moderate spread of shot, he gritted his teeth and squeezed the trigger. The powder in the pan ignited first, and then with a tremendous roar and truly spectacular muzzle flash, the Nock delivered a kick like a mule. But that was nothing to the devastation it had created.

Deliberately aimed low, seven heavy balls spread out and tore into the looming animals, bringing them and their riders crashing to the ground. As though struck by a giant mallet, the whole war party momentarily plunged about in chaos before resuming the attack. Taking advantage of the brief respite, Bannock finished reloading and again levelled his long rifle.

Ignoring the terrific ache in his shoulder, Butler dropped the smoking and now thoroughly redundant volleygun, and grabbed his two percussion pistols. As the Comanches finally reached the trench, three more shots ripped into them. This time the hot lead was unleashed at almost point-blank range into human flesh and blood. Screams rent the night air, as mutilated bodies toppled from their ponies. Such was the accumulated death toll that, had the Comanches not been so close, they would probably have broken off the attack. Unlike the white man, they were rarely prepared to tolerate heavy casualties merely to gain victory. As it was, however, momentum and blind rage carried them forwards, so they suddenly swarmed over the two defenders.

Grasping his Hawken by its long barrel, Bannock viciously swung the weapon around, all the while howling like a berserker. Confronted by a solid mass of men and animals, he just couldn't miss. The Comanches' numbers were actually counting against them – and yet still they didn't dismount, because fighting on foot simply wasn't in their nature. Unable to draw their bows in such a mêlée, instead the warriors lashed out with clubs, and stabbed down with their war lances.

Bannock's arm painfully absorbed a jarring crash, as

his rifle's stock collided with another victim. Swearing obscenely, Butler hurled his empty pistols at the heaving mob, and then unsheathed a long-bladed knife. Rising up to his full height, he slashed back and forth in a lateral arc. The finely honed blade sliced through flesh and muscle, so that screams of pain vied with war cries for ascendancy. For a short time the defenders' sheer ferocity held back the great mass of Indians. Then Set-tainte and a few others were able to manoeuvre on to the white men's flanks, and notch their arrows.

Abruptly recognizing that the situation was hopeless, Bannock yelled out, 'Run for it, Chet. It's our only hope.' Still he hadn't drawn his Colts: in the midst of such frenzied hand-to-hand fighting, he just hadn't had the opportunity.

'You first. I'll hold 'em off,' Butler bellowed back.

Grabbing hold of a spare powder flask, Bannock turned and powered up out of the trench. His intention was to ascend the small rise and then cover his friend's retreat with revolver fire. But then the inevitable happened. Now alone, Butler simply couldn't cover every angle. A lance point penetrated his right thigh, and went deep. Very deep.

Moaning with pain, the massive scout only just managed to stay on his feet. Hurling his knife at his assailant, he had the momentary pleasure of seeing it enter the Comanche's belly like a skewer. Drawing in a full breath, he hollered, 'Haul ass, Bannock. They've kilt me!'

For a brief moment Bannock watched as the Indians,

still believing Butler to be dangerous, swarmed over his friend. 'I'm mighty sorry I got you into this,' he muttered, and then took off as though the hounds of hell were pursuing him. Sounds of a fleeting struggle followed on, and then the Comanches uttered a collective shriek of triumph, which could only have signified Chet Butler's bloody demise.

CHAPTER THREE

Set-tainte angrily scrutinized the dark and bloody ground leading up to the concealed trench. The totally unexpected battle had been short, but incredibly vicious. Men and animals, both dead and terribly wounded, lay at staggered intervals. The ponies would end up being eaten, whilst those survivors that could travel would be taken back to their temporary base camp in the north-east, to be tended by the women. There would be much wailing and self-mutilation in remembrance of the fallen.

His gaze switched to the disfigured corpse of the huge white man. Ideally, Set-tainte would have preferred him taken alive so as to ascertain his identity, and also to exact some satisfaction with long hours of excruciating torture. Unfortunately, in the frenzy of the moment, he had been perceived as too lethal by far, and death had been the only solution. The question was, who were these ferocious fighters? Could it be that they belonged to the hated and feared *Tejano* Rangers?

After grimly spitting a great gobbet of phlegm into

the dust, the war chief pondered his next move. Despite this particular setback, the raid had still been a great success. They had captured much valuable livestock, and many women and children. Those of the latter they didn't choose to keep would undoubtedly be welcomed in trade by the New Mexican Comancheros. Therefore Set-tainte's prime responsibility had to be to get them all on the move, along with the injured. And yet he also couldn't allow the second white man to escape: that one would definitely have to scream out his prolonged death agonies in front of the whole tribe. Abruptly he came to a decision. He could certainly spare ten warriors, and that many mounted men had to be enough to hunt down one lone fugitive on foot.

A long, tormented scream came from over near the now smouldering wagons. His men had returned to the pleasurable task at hand. It might not prove that easy to persuade some of them to break off and pursue a still dangerous white man, but it *would* happen. Set-tainte needed to obtain retribution, and he possessed enough prestige to enforce his wishes. He had also decided that the fearsome volleygun would be his. A weapon of such destructive power could only enhance his position in the tribe. The bone-crushing practicalities of actually firing the piece could wait for another time.

Like so many of his race, the Comanche chief was an unprepossessing figure when viewed on foot. Short and scrawny, there was nothing to indicate his consummate ability to control the vast territory that his people held in such a vicelike grip. Because it was an indisputable fact that mounted on fleet-footed ponies, he and all his kind had no equal as light cavalry. Such deadly skill had been enough to stop the Spanish in their northward quest for empire. That wasn't to say, however, that they couldn't be beaten in a fight.

After long decades of total dominance, the horse Indians had found themselves confronted by a new and deadly foe, armed with repeating weapons. And over the course of the last few years, formerly unheard of reverses had occurred on many occasions in parts of West Texas. Which was why, even as he began mentally to construct his pursuit party, a certain niggling uneasiness refused to leave the dark recesses of his mind.

With his breath coming in short, rasping gasps and his legs turning to jelly, Bannock reluctantly slowed to a walk. There was little point in driving himself to exhaustion. And yet, knowing that pursuit was almost inevitable, he kept glancing back over his shoulder. The first streaks of daylight were showing in the east. It surely couldn't be long before they came pounding after him. So it was that, as he trudged across the increasingly broken ground, he made a careful scrutiny of his immediate surroundings. Even as he did so, he was able to reload his long rifle, mostly by feel alone.

The land that he was moving into was no longer just featureless desert, or rolling open grassland of the type so favourable to horse Indians. Liberally dotted about with massive Saguaro cacti, it contained rock-strewn rises and bone-dry arroyos carved out by periodic flash floods. All of these features could assist him, come the time of his next desperate battle for survival.

It was just as well that he remained pre-occupied, because otherwise it was quite likely that he would have been overcome with guilt over the death of his only real friend. Since no one could deliver a verdict on whether the two of them would have been discovered or not, he could only assume that his unilateral action had been the sole cause. And for what? To carry out a mercy killing on a child he didn't even know? Perhaps that, too, had been brought about by guilt. The guilt of not being able to save that child in the first place. After all, he had supposedly signed on to keep them all out of trouble. Really it was just too painful to think about, and best kept locked away until a time when he was no longer in imminent danger. Nevertheless, some things are easier decided on than carried out.

As a great surge of uncontrollable emotion welled up inside him, he suddenly cried out in anguish. 'Sweet Jesus, what have I done?'

His answer to that came promptly, and from a most unwelcome source. The distinctive sound of fast-moving riders broke in on his tormented thoughts. These unwanted visitors could only have come from the stricken wagon train. In truth, it was amazing that the Comanches had taken so long. Then again, they had doubtless had a great many women to rape!

Anxiously searching for sanctuary, Bannock spied a jumble of modest boulders off to his left. They weren't much, but they'd have to suffice. Guilty thoughts temporarily left him, for it was entirely possible that he would shortly be joining his friend in hell . . . or wherever men like them ended up!

Although knowing that he had to have been spotted, Bannock moved over to his latest defensive position at a deliberately measured pace. There was fear in his heart a-plenty, but also years of hard-won experience to fall back on. If he was going to produce accurate fire, then he needed to avoid any heavy exertion.

Upon reaching the dubious safety of the waist-high boulders, he knelt down behind one and laid his Hawken on the top of it. Just as on the day before, a chill came over him as he studied his opponents. The menacing group had come to a halt a couple of hundred yards away. There were exactly ten of them. They were well spaced out, and didn't seem in any all-fired hurry to come to blows. Apaches would have dismounted and crept up on him, skilfully utilizing the available cover, but that wasn't the Comanches' way.

'Probably recalling the last time they took a run at me,' Bannock muttered dryly to steady his fluttering nerves.

Since in reality the warriors were most probably pondering their plan of attack, Bannock had no intention of allowing them that luxury. He wanted to force the pace. Cocking his rifle, he carefully drew a bead on one of the centremost Indians. After squeezing the rear trigger, the front one required only the lightest caress. Breathing in, he suddenly held it and fired.

For an experienced marksman, the result was never in doubt. The ball struck his victim left of centre, penetrating the man's heart and instantly snuffing out his life. As the warrior toppled backwards off his pony, the others reacted predictably. They knew that their enemy would have to reload before firing again, and so had to reach him first. Splitting into two groups, they vigorously urged their animals up to speed. Five of them swept around Bannock's right flank, whilst the remainder charged directly for him. The Comanches' intention was obvious: they were out to catch him in a pincer movement, except that because his murderous intervention had provoked them into premature action, their timing was now hopelessly askew.

Temporarily ignoring their approach, he commenced recharging the muzzle-loader. Instinctively he knew that he wouldn't get the chance to fire it again before the first of them reached him, but it could well come in useful in the aftermath. Providing, of course, that he survived the attack!

As it happened, he didn't get time to replace the percussion cap, because the nearest group of four was almost upon him. Leaning the long gun against a boulder, he drew both Paterson Colts from his belt. As he thumbed back the hammers, a retractable trigger dropped down from inside each frame. This was the testing time. Because he hadn't yet used his revolvers, Bannock hoped that they would come as a lethal surprise to his assailants.

Although acutely aware of the second group swinging around behind him, the lone defender consciously ignored them. Holding his fire until the oncoming Comanches were merely yards away, he abruptly levelled both weapons.

'God save me from misfires!' he fervently exclaimed.

Aiming at the riders rather than their ponies, he

fired first the left-hand, and then the right-hand weapon. As the Colts bucked in his clutches, two .36 calibre balls slammed into naked flesh in rapid succession. One warrior, about to hurl his lance, fell uncontrollably sideways from his mount. Another grunted and doubled over in pain, the cheap trader musket that he had been about to fire slipping from his grasp.

As a hastily loosed arrow ricocheted off the boulder behind which he sheltered, Bannock tilted both revolvers to right angles, so allowing any fragments of the copper percussion caps to drop clear of the workings. Believing that their foe needed to reload, the two uninjured bucks urged their ponies up the short rise, directly at him. For the solitary white man, this was truly a test of nerve!

Knowing that he still had four chambers left in each weapon, Bannock again levelled them and fired. From the left-hand gun there was merely a muted pop, but mercifully the right-hand one belched forth death. The ball tore away the Comanche's lower jaw, leaving him flailing about in agony. Horrified at the continued shooting, his surviving companion turned tail and raced to safety. Seemingly this warrior never even considered joining his compatriots on the other flank. Had he been the only one left, Bannock would have attempted to 'nail' him with the Hawken, but from the noise behind him, he knew that the second war party was almost upon him. Turning to confront the new threat, he again readied his Colts.

The pain that suddenly erupted in his left side was

excruciating. Glancing down, he saw an arrow shaft protruding from his worn clothing. At that point, his desperate battle for survival was on a cusp. Pain and shock could overwhelm him, leading to his ending up staked out on an anthill with his pecker in his mouth, or. . . .

Or he could get real mad. And that's what happened. Snarling out his defiance, he swung both Colts towards the packed horsemen and indiscriminately opened fire. Each receiving mortal wounds, two ponies buckled beneath their riders, throwing them heavily. Then twice more, Bannock cocked and fired the revolvers, killing one warrior stone dead, and painfully wounding another. As a significant cloud of sulphurous smoke drifted over the killing ground, only one Comanche remained mounted and untouched. And he couldn't possibly know that the apparently crazed white man was now actually holding empty weapons.

Manically screaming out his bloodlust, Bannock cocked and aimed both Colts at the dismayed warrior, whose nerve promptly deserted him. Brutally yanking on the reins, he turned his pony and raced away without once looking back. That left two warriors stunned on the ground, and one bleeding profusely from a badly gashed forehead. With blood masking his vision, and struggling to remain mounted, he wasn't an immediate threat.

Discarding the belt guns, Bannock unsheathed his Bowie knife and unsteadily advanced on the temporarily helpless Indians. Without any compunction, he shuffled from one to the other, entwining his fingers in buffalo-greased hair and then viciously slicing through their exposed carotid arteries. As their lifeblood flowed into the dirt, the bodies briefly twitched feverishly before falling still. Then, standing amongst the cadavers, with blood dripping from both his massive blade and his wounded side, he peered up at the sole remaining warrior.

It was this hellish vision that that individual witnessed when he finally wiped the blood from his eyes, and any thoughts of continued aggression instantly left him. Digging his heels in, the terrified Comanche rode past Bannock at speed, following the other two fleeing warriors in the general direction of the burnt-out wagon train.

As the realization hit home that he had actually survived, a great tremor passed through Bannock's body. Then he felt his legs beginning to wobble. The twin forces of reaction and blood loss were taking effect, but he couldn't afford to surrender to them just yet. Of the first wave of assailants, three had definitely taken gunshot wounds, but any number of them might still pose a threat.

Unsteadily he wiped his knife blade clean on the breechclout of his nearest victim. Then, staggering back up to his original position, Bannock retrieved his rifle and pressed a fresh percussion cap on to the nipple. Leaning against the boulder, he carefully scrutinized his victims. 'Broken jaw' was quite obviously alive, but in so much torment that he was totally incapacitated by it. The buck that he had shot first had a blood-soaked hole directly over his heart and was

41

quite obviously dead. That left the fellow with the musket. He appeared to have been gut shot, but such an injury could take time to kill a man, leaving him in the meantime mad, bad, and infinitely dangerous to approach.

Not wishing to waste powder unnecessarily, Bannock decided to move in a little closer. He had a hankering for the powder flask hanging by a rawhide thong from the warrior's neck. Groaning from the pain in his side, he cautiously advanced down the low rise. He had barely covered three paces when the wounded Comanche suddenly exploded from the ground in a strange crablike movement. Although hampered by the ball in his belly, the knife in his hand presented a deadly threat that could only be answered in one way.

Swiftly raising the Hawken, Bannock contracted his right forefinger, hard, and watched with relief as his enemy's skull exploded like a ripe melon. Glancing up at the horizon, he spotted one of the three fugitives momentarily rein in and glance back, before quickly resuming his headlong flight. Grunting, the ailing white man knew that he had to finish the business swiftly, before he passed out. Seizing his rifle by its barrel, he staggered over to 'broken jaw'. That pathetic creature was on his knees in a world of hurt, and didn't even look up. His cold-eyed nemesis twice slammed the butt into the side of the helpless individual's head with great force. Only then did he permit himself to sink to the ground and close his eyes.

Anybody happening upon him now would find easy

pickings indeed, but there could be no help for that. Because the man known only as Bannock had temporarily exceeded even his formidable limits!

CHAPTER FOUR

Little Pepita felt unaccustomed apprehension as she stared around the vast adobe settlement that she knew as home. Although only young, she already possessed the dubious ability of being able to sense the mood of her father and other adults. And what she perceived was both strange and unsettling. Ever since the summer moon had begun to grow large in the night sky, a peculiar dread seemed to have settled over them. They constantly watched the horizon, shaking their heads and muttering darkly. No longer was the spirited girl allowed to stray far from the buildings. It was all very puzzling.

The Catholic mission station of San Marcos, named after a particularly devoted and resolute priest, had at one time been a thriving centre of agriculture and religious observance. But after only a few blissful years of tranquillity, it had been discovered by a party of roving Comanches, and shortly afterwards the raids had started. At first, as though testing the defences, they just involved the theft of animals. But then women and children were carried off, followed by warriors brazenly riding into the mission demanding ransom for their return. The marauding Indians could quite easily have slaughtered all the steadfastly passive inhabitants, but deliberately chose not to, because the mission's tenuous survival allowed them to continue with their annual depredations.

Far to the south, in Mexico City, the venal individuals who happened to be clinging to power at the time weren't prepared to spare the soldiers so desperately required to defend the remote settlement. And so, finally, the priests reluctantly accepted the inevitable. San Marcos was abandoned.

Yet in a forgotten land, where nothing came easily, the presence of a ready-made habitation could not long be ignored, and gradually, after a few years, some of Sonora's dirt-poor peons claimed the place for themselves. The once strong walls had crumbled in places, but enough remained to provide shelter and a semblance of protection. The small church, once a place of quiet worship, had succumbed to more practical purposes. As the coolest building, it was now used as a storeroom, and its parishioners were more likely to be wandering chickens. Water, the most precious of all resources, was readily available from a nearby arroyo. With a good supply of labour, the irrigation ditches were resurrected.

Of course the return of a little civilization to San Marcos was inevitably discovered. And so, inexorably, the earlier cycle began to repeat itself, because the capacity for resistance of the mission's new occupants was little better than that of their predecessors. Up until now that had just involved the theft of livestock, but as before all would soon change.

Pepita knew none of this, because her father had taken the foolish decision not to spoil her short childhood with such alarming stories. Headstrong and tomboyish, she just desired the freedom to roam beyond the immediate confines of the settlement's buildings. And, petulantly stamping her small, tanned foot in the dirt, she abruptly determined that the next day she would do exactly that!

Set-tainte stared at the three shamefaced survivors with a mixture of anger and disbelief. Disgracefully, two were completely unharmed, whereas at least the third was liberally coated with his own blood. Discounting some of the obviously embellished descriptions, the chief pieced together the fact that their lone opponent was lean and tanned, almost like a Comanche, but far taller. *And* he carried the pistols that fired many times. Just like the hated *Tejano* Rangers.

Since it was quite out of the question to send yet more warriors after this cursed individual, he could only hope that they would come across him on one of their future forays. As it was, they needed to get the surviving captives and all their plunder back up to the temporary holding camp southwest of the Rio Bravo. Only then could he lead his warriors out on further raids. As it happened, the war chief had a particularly tempting village in mind that his warriors had so far only toyed with. The time had come to really exact some tribute!

'May you all burn in hell, you heathen bastards!' screamed out one of the captive white women through swollen lips, all innocence and tolerance now long since dissipated. Such was her ruined condition that she couldn't recognize the incongruity of her desperate protest. The momentary defiance was reduced to a whimper by her new master's rawhide whip, with yet another livid welt appearing on her much abused flesh.

Set-tainte had no idea what she had just said, and nor did he care. She would need all her apparent spirit just to survive the next few days. Raising an arm, he signalled for the now bloated war party to move out. Two heavily laden wagons, containing food and various items of clothing and furniture that had appealed to their whimsical tastes, accompanied them. As the great caravan moved off, all that remained of the Children of God's great odyssey were the charred fittings of burnt-out wagons and the bodies of the slain, now food for the carrion birds that had inevitably gathered. As the noise of the departing procession diminished, these loathsome creatures began tearing at the corpse nearest to them, which also happened to be the largest by far.

Chet Butler's features were no longer recognizably human, but that counted for nothing to the black vultures that tore at his flesh. He and the wagon train's many other victims would keep the birds occupied for a long time, unless they were driven off by other, larger predators. And yet they were not the only meal in the offing!

47

*

It was the sudden weight on his stomach that finally woke him. That and the stabbing pain in his side. As Bannock's eyelids snapped open, he beheld a pair of expressionless eyes directly facing him. A short, viciously hooked beak was poised to tear at the blood-stained clothing that had initially attracted the vile thing.

'Get away from me, you bastard!' he barked out, as he reached for his knife.

Unsurprisingly he didn't need to use it, as the vulture preferred food that was already dead. It was its misfortune to have picked on the only participant of the fight still breathing. Alarmed, the bird rapidly flapped out of sight – but the injured man knew full well that it could only be a matter of time before others of its ilk, *and* far more dangerous four-legged scavengers appeared.

Cautiously, Bannock scrutinized his surroundings. It was now late afternoon, and amazingly he appeared to be all alone. But he couldn't be certain he would remain like that. It all depended on how badly the Comanches wanted his scalp. So he needed to cover some distance before nightfall. Sadly, all the ponies belonging to his victims had wandered off. He would have to walk . . . if he was able.

Tentatively he examined his wound. The bleeding appeared to have ceased, mainly due to the fact that the arrow was still lodged in it. Gritting his teeth, he gave the shaft an exploratory tug. The pain was excruciating, the benefit non-existent. His only reward was to see fresh blood coating the shaft.

'God's bones, that won't answer!' he exclaimed.

It was grimly apparent that he couldn't both extract the arrow *and* expect to travel. The former gruelling procedure would have to wait. Sighing, he took the next best course. Gripping the greasy shaft with both hands, he abruptly snapped it in half. The resulting agony nearly caused him to pass out again. Beads of sweat welled up on his forehead, as he allowed the severed end to fall from his trembling fingers.

Minutes passed before he again opened his eyes. This was no good. He needed to be on his way. With a supreme effort, Bannock rolled first on to his right side, and then on to all fours. Putting off the ultimate effort for a few moments longer, he crawled over to where the musket-owning Comanche lay. Greedily the white man seized the large flask of black powder from around his neck. Whether it was of Du Pont quality was questionable, but it would undoubtedly come in handy. As an afterthought, he also decided to take the musket, and in addition a buffalo-hide pouch containing lead balls. It would add to his firepower, and he could also now have a long gun on either side, to act as walking supports.

Next, after painfully getting to his feet, he recovered his own firearms. Fighting the strong desire to be on the move, he undertook the laborious task of reloading them. Since they were all in effect muzzleloaders, the process involved both time and discomfort. Only then did he finally depart. After some thought he had determined to head east, on the assumption that such a route would likely keep him away from the Comanche war party.

Bannock knew full well that his continued survival depended on two things. Somehow he had to obtain another mount, *and* his wound would, at some point, require concerted attention if he was to avoid greenrod setting in. As he trudged away from the broken bodies of his enemies, the lone white man was under no illusions as to the odds stacked against him. All he had on his side was the ability to endure . . . and a great deal of grit!

As he glanced back at the slow-moving column, the possible presence of hostile Indians was the last thing on *Coronel* Vallejo's mind. His force of two hundred and fifty regulars was the closest thing that Mexico had to an 'Army of the North', but his men hadn't trudged all this way just to punish some mangy Comanche raiders.

That was probably a good thing, because in truth the infantry, although able to defend themselves well enough against attack, would have stood no chance of pursuing and tackling horse Indians.

The *coronel* had been personally charged by His Excellency *Presidente* Jose Herrera to proceed immediately to Northern California, where he was to assist Governor Pio Pico in repelling the unwelcome advances of certain *Americanos* from the east. It was no secret that the United States of America coveted the rich and juicy province of California, but it was not to be theirs . . . not yet, anyway!

For long moments, Vallejo was lost in thought, as he

contemplated the joyous prospect of hurling the damn *gringos* back across the Sierras, and then returning home to great acclaim. He had little interest in Mexico's far-flung empire, and dearly missed the comforts of the capital, but he had been assigned to this loathsome task by the highest in the land, and so had no choice other than to comply. Besides, a successful outcome would surely guarantee his advancement to the glorious rank of general.

Hearing hoofbeats, he came to his senses in time to see the approach of Capitan Ugalde. From the expression on that individual's handsome features, the dark-haired young officer obviously had something more on his mind than just absent pleasures. There was something unsettlingly capable about the *capitan* that uncomfortably reminded Vallejo of his own professional shortcomings. Whenever real soldiering was called for, he became acutely aware that his advancement so far had had a lot to do with family influence rather than real ability.

Reining in next to his commander, Ugalde proffered a perfunctory salute, and immediately came to the point. 'By my reckoning, we have now passed out of Chihuahua and into Sonora, *mi coronel.*'

'What of it?' that man responded sharply. It had not been his intention to be brusque, but the relentless heat in this accursed province was causing his head to ache abominably. It really was a sad fact that he was singularly ill used to the rigours of campaigning.

The *capitan* favoured him with a cautious smile. 'Only that we have made good time today, and the men are almost exhausted,' he pointedly replied. 'Perhaps we could make camp earlier tonight.'

Vallejo grunted non-committedly. 'You're a strange one, Ugalde. You must be the only officer that I have served with to be concerned about the wellbeing of his men. I heard that Santa Anna once compared the lives of his *soldados* to those of so many chickens, and in all probability that attitude will be the same throughout the whole of Mexico.'

The *capitan* sighed. 'Perhaps that's why the general is now in exile, señor. All I know is that we may have to depend on those *chickens* some day soon, and I'd rather have them shooting at our enemies than our backs.'

That tickled his superior. 'Hah! Put like that, you may just have a point. Very well. You may select a suitable campsite.' Mopping the sweat from his forehead, he added, 'And I don't mind telling you, *capitan*, that after putting me through this ordeal, any accursed Yankees that we run across are going to suffer gravely. Whether they are in California or not!'

One particular Yankee was already suffering quite badly enough. Although night had finally fallen, Bannock still doggedly stumbled along, a long gun gripped tightly in each hand, like walking sticks to steady his progress over the uneven ground. Somewhere in the recesses of his mind an insistent voice was telling him to lie down, but he knew that if he succumbed he might never get up again. *And* it was cooler now that the burning sun had gone down. *And* he desperately wanted to put more distance between the last contact point with the Comanches. And. . .

For the umpteenth time pain seared through his left side, and he was unable to contain a loud groan. Bannock was dismally aware that blood was seeping steadily from it. If he weren't careful, it would be that relatively mediocre injury that killed him!

The butt of his Hawken struck a rock, and almost immediately he heard a terrifyingly distinctive rattling sound, a short distance off to his left. Knowing full well what that portended, he twisted sharply away. His intention was to make a wide detour around the dangerous reptile, but his ill-used body simply refused to comply. His left foot caught on another rock, and this time he crashed to the hard, unyielding ground. Winded and befuddled, he lay like a stranded whale. Hard-learned frontier instincts screamed at him to get up, but it was not to be. His eyes began to lose focus, and his limbs just wouldn't answer. The last word that he uttered before blackness overwhelmed him was, 'Chet!'

Pepita giggled with childish delight. She had eluded her father and was beyond the confines of San Marcos's adobe walls. Lacking a mother, she tended to have less supervision than the other children, although on this occasion not even her friends knew where she was. The fact that she carried no food or water never even registered in her mind seething with excitement. Extending before the eager ten-year-old were limitless opportunities for adventure, not least because on this side of the former mission station the terrain was exceptionally inhospitable. There was no cultivation and no livestock. Just scrub desert and rocks. Bounding eagerly forwards, the little girl made first for a great Saguaro cactus that seemed particularly appealing to her. She had heard that it contained a delightfully juicy liquid.

As her deeply tanned legs skipped lightly over the gritty sand, her favourite cotton dress flowed around her body. It was really too small for her growing frame, but nothing on earth would make her forsake it. Taking a great deal of time and trouble, her mother had dyed it red using the juice from crushed berries. She was the only child in the settlement to possess such a colourful item of clothing. The fact that she could be spotted miles away wasn't something that would trouble her young mind.

It was only when she got really close to the cactus that it abruptly lost all its charms. Long, vicious-looking spines that seemed to be almost eager to hurt her, protruded from it. The disappointment was fleeting however, because Pepita then noticed a great Barrel cactus that appeared less well defended. As she turned eagerly towards it, two things happened that someone of her tender years could never have foreseen.

From off to her right came a rattling sound that she knew only too well. Snakes were no respecter of walls, and had even bitten unwary people in the settlement. This particular one reared up into view, fastening its emotionless eyes on to her, and causing the little girl to freeze with fear. And what occurred next was, in its own way, even more terrifying. With her peripheral vision, she witnessed a huge, bloodstained and bearded apparition emerge from behind a rock. In its right hand was a gun that suddenly belched out smoke and flame. Reacting instinctively, Pepita unleashed a high-pitched scream that continued long after the mangled rattlesnake had collapsed to the ground.

There was a rush of bodies from the settlement. Knowing full well the dangers that existed, the men were fearful but determined. Most carried knives or staves. Only one possessed a firearm, and that was a flintlock of very dubious quality. What they could actually have achieved against serious danger was anybody's guess, and thankfully they weren't to be tested. Pepita's cries made her easy to locate, and the scene before them told the whole story. The dead rattlesnake elicited both surprise and relief, but the sight of its killer, lying under a dissipating cloud of smoke, stopped them in their tracks.

'Papa!' wailed Pepita, as she rushed into his arms.

For a long moment, the young Mexican enveloped her in a great hug, before abruptly releasing her. 'Did it bite you, little one?' he demanded, his eyes anxiously scrutinizing her arms and legs.

'No. It didn't get the chance,' she replied, keen to return to the comforting embrace. All thoughts of adventure had left her. Her only concern now was to somehow avoid the inevitable scolding, and thankfully there was a good chance. 'That man saved me!' she eagerly announced.

With the little girl obviously safe, the villagers, some ten in number, transferred their full attention to the prone stranger. Cautiously, they advanced towards him. Their eyes took in his various weapons, but what really caught their interest was the blood-soaked wound in his left side.

'*Bandido*?' one of the men muttered nervously.

It was Pepita's father who discovered the truth. Kneeling down, he carefully moved the clothing until the remaining section of arrow shaft was visible.

Another villager inhaled rapidly and stepped back. Making the sign of the cross, that man announced, 'Apache, or maybe Seri.'

At that instant, Bannock's eyelids snapped open and he barked out one word, 'Comanche!'

That brought a collective chill to the group. '*Madre de Dios*!' another exclaimed. 'Has he brought them to us?'

'If he had, they would be here now,' Pepita's father opined sharply. 'As it is, he saved my daughter. So the least I can do is tend his wound and feed him. Help me carry him inside.'

None of the men moved. Instead they merely glanced uncertainly at each other. 'He's a *gringo*,' the fellow who had crossed himself remarked. 'Which means he is nothing to us.'

Pepita's father was scathing. 'So we leave him here to die, and then rob his body? Is that his reward for shooting the snake?' Angrily he glanced from one to the other. 'You make me sick. Well, I'll carry him in alone then. Just watch.'

His words had an effect. Communal embarrassment set in, and finally they lent a hand. As he again drifted into unconsciousness, Bannock was vaguely aware of being lifted from the ground and carried away. By the time that he entered the grounds of San Marcos he was totally oblivious to his new surroundings.

CHAPTER FIVE

Bannock opened his eyes slowly. The room was dark and peaceful, and apparently free of menace. He lay on a low cot, and amazingly his body felt relaxed and unfettered by pain. Tentatively he touched his left side. The severed arrow shaft, and hopefully the head also, were gone. All that remained was some form of bandage, tightly wrapped around his stomach.

Cautiously, he lifted his head and peered around. Even in such seemingly tranquil circumstances, he did not take anything for granted. Had he woken naturally, or had there been some other reason? There, in the shadows, he could just make out a red object. It suddenly moved, and his heart rate leapt. That in turn touched off a slight spasm in his side, which told him one thing. His wound had been tended to, but hadn't yet healed.

The suddenly cornered white man feverishly reached around for a weapon. *Any* kind of weapon. Then, abruptly, he realized that he didn't need one. Sighing with relief, he watched as a little girl approached him. Even in the poor light, it was obvious that she wasn't a Comanche child. Smiling nervously, she moved to his side. Only then did he begin to recall having seen her in the recent past.

'You killed the snake before it could bite me,' she remarked quietly, in heavily accented English. 'That means you must be my friend.'

Bannock twitched with surprise, as the memory of that event flooded back. 'I guess I must be, little lady. So tell me, how come you speak such good American?'

She gazed at him very seriously. 'That's because my . . .'

The door suddenly opened wide, allowing more light to flood into the room, and a man entered. That he was angry was obvious. He spoke sharply in Spanish, and the girl ran out without another word. Then he turned to his prone guest and began to speak in halting English.

'Pepita is my . . . daughter. She knows you have been hurt, and should not, how you say, annoy you?'

Bannock looked closely at the Mexican. Slim and of medium height and build, he appeared to be about thirty years old, although such things could be hard to tell. People aged quickly in such a land. One thing was obvious, however, to someone who knew what to look for. His face was open and honest, with no sign of meanness or latent aggression. The features were those of a simple peon, who spent his days trying to extract a living from the harsh surroundings.

'No call for you to get wrathy with her, mister,' the American softly remarked. 'Happen she just wanted to say hello, is all.'

It was obvious that his host was struggling with some of the mangled dialogue, but nevertheless he replied, 'There are many things I would know, *señor.*'

Bannock smiled. 'Likewise. But let's start with names, huh? Those that know me, call me Bannock.' And with that he reached out his right hand.

The Mexican readily accepted the grip. 'My name is Luis. I live in this simple place with my daughter.' He paused and looked closely at his guest. 'I do not wish to, ah . . . press you, *señor*, but word of that arrow wound has spread. People here are nervous. I would know what happened to you in the desert.'

Bannock nodded. He could well understand their apprehension. Deciding that complete honesty was the best way, he related slowly and graphically just what had befallen him. Although Luis listened in stunned silence, the terrible fate of the wagon train left him with eyes as wide as saucers. Even if he hadn't always understood every word, he was left in no doubt as to the dreadful sequence of events that had transpired. And that gave rise to a very grave question indeed.

'Could it be that you have led them to us, Señor Bannock? If they were to follow your tracks.'

That man emphatically shook his head. 'Nah. Not a chance. If they had wanted another crack at me, they'd have come after me again and caught up for sure. But the thing is, Comanches don't like taking casualties. It unnerves them. So if those sons of bitches do happen to turn up at this settlement, it's because they already know that you're here.' He returned Luis's searching gaze. '*Do* they know of this place?'

The younger man shrugged slightly, but couldn't hide his discomfort. 'Things have happened. Animals stolen in the night. We never saw who did it.'

Bannock's eyes were like gimlets. 'And did you even go looking?'

Shrugging, Luis reluctantly shook his head. 'We are peaceful people, *señor*. We have few weapons. What could we have done?'

It was the American's turn to shrug. 'Got yourselves kilt, probably. But however you look at it, you failed the test.'

'*Que?*'

'You didn't show any fight. Which means that whoever stole them animals will be sure to return for a bigger piece of pie.'

Luis's confusion was very evident. '*Piece of pie?*'

Bannock just smiled tolerantly and abruptly changed the subject. 'How come you and Pepita speak American so good?'

It was the Mexican's turn to display sadness. 'I married a woman from Texas. She died of fever one year ago. I was *mucho* in love with her. Pepita has her beauty, which for me is good . . . and yet sometimes not so good. It reminds me of what we have lost.'

Bannock suddenly thought of the little girl that he had shot near the burning wagons. 'Children sure as hell get a rough deal in this country,' he opined, his features suddenly grim. Then, in an effort to lighten the mood, he asked, 'Just how long have I been laying here, anyhu?'

Luis appeared startled. It hadn't occurred to him that his guest didn't know. 'Three days, *señor*. It was as well that you slept. Pulling out the arrowhead took *mucho*, how you say . . . effort. There was great blood.'

'Three days!' Bannock exclaimed. 'No wonder I could eat a horse. That's if those thieving varmints left you any,' he added slyly.

The peon smiled. 'We have only simple fair, but what is mine is also yours. Can you walk with me?'

Bannock carefully eased his body from the cot, grunting a little, as he got upright. 'If there's vittles on offer, I'll walk any distance, my friend.' He wasn't to know, as he followed his host from the room, that hostile Indians weren't the only people out for a piece of pie!

After impatiently wiping his sweat from the eyepiece of the drawtube spyglass, *Coronel* Vallejo returned his attention to the sprawling adobe mission. Compared to many of the structures in Mexico City it wasn't much to look at, but it *was* the largest settlement that he'd seen since entering Sonora. It even seemed to possess a small church, although he very much doubted if there was still a priest in residence. With its disintegrating walls and almost non-existent gates, San Marcos was certainly no fortress – but that was of no concern to Vallejo. He wasn't there to fight, merely to sample their hospitality.

Glancing at his companion, he drily remarked, 'It appears that the inhabitants of this Godforsaken furnace will soon have the pleasure of feeding us all. And for that they will briefly enjoy our protection. After

62

all, is that not why we accepted our commissions as officers and gentlemen?'

Capitan Ugalde peered around at the apparently deserted terrain. 'Protection from what, *mi coronel?*'

His commanding officer laughed cynically. 'Very probably some of the gutter sweepings behind us.'

Ugalde shrugged. Despite his earnest attempts to treat the enlisted men as human beings, he sadly recognized that many of them fell far below such a generous categorization, and that appearances could be deceptive. Because, although dusty and sweat stained, the column of tramping soldiers was undeniably impressive, and very deliberately so. Their blue uniforms, fronted by white cross belts, were reminiscent of the Napoleonic era. The tall, cylindrical caps known as shakos endowed the men with the illusion of great height. The only concession to the scorching sun was a black visor at the front of each shako, though that afforded little real protection.

The two senior mounted officers, and more especially the *coronel*, were even more splendidly outfitted. His blue tunic boasted gold and scarlet facings, and gleaming bullion epaulettes. More gold trim ran around the collars and cuffs. On their heads, both sported bicorn hats, running front to rear. Down the column, even the assorted *tenientes* were easily distinguishable from the common soldiers by the fact that they, too, were mounted.

Although completely impractical on the frontier, the intention behind such a garish display of finery was to overawe the troublesome Yankees and return some order to the Mexican possession of California. And nothing emphasized that aim more than the numerous red, white and green flags on show.

Unfortunately, such military might was often little more than vain bravado. The rank and file mostly consisted of unhappy conscripts, drawn from the prisons and starving unemployed. That they weren't always either motivated or well led had been amply demonstrated in the war with the Texicans in the previous decade. Their apparent discipline was little more than a brittle shell, soon shattered in the presence of temptation. And what could be more tempting than a remote settlement containing women? Because it was a sure thing that not all of them would be wrinkled old crones!

Bannock sat before an open fire, contentedly devouring a plate of tortillas and beans. A mug of steaming coffee, or what passed for it in such a place, awaited his attention. So immense was his hunger that the plain meal seemed fit for a president, and he didn't even notice the villagers observing him apprehensively. They were simple folk, who had heard only bad things about the aggressive, foul-mouthed *gringos* from the north.

His feasting was so single-minded that he unintentionally ignored little Pepita, as the girl settled down opposite him. Her eyes registered great curiosity. Never before had she seen anyone remotely like this lean stranger. She couldn't conceivably have put such thoughts into words, but he had the look of a predator. Dangerous and yet apparently benign, because after all he had quite possibly saved her life. The child had all sorts of questions, but something about his demeanour constrained her. And yet ... the impetuosity that had sent her out into the desert alone began to reassert itself. Opening her mouth, she was just about to speak, when a voice bellowed out from the entrance to the compound.

'*Madre de dios*! Riders coming, and men on foot. Many, many men.'

Bannock hadn't understood the warning, but the startled reaction of those around him sufficed. Cramming in another mouthful, he reluctantly got to his feet to wait on events. The effort made him wince from the pain in his side, but he decided that it was tolerable, and indeed far better than before.

It was Luis who asked the question that was on everyone's mind, forgetting for a moment that marauding Indians never went anywhere on foot. 'Indios?'

'No. *Soldados.*'

There was a rush for the entrance. Many of the peons crossed themselves at the sight of the approaching soldiers. It seemed that no one expected them to be benign visitors.

'We have some reason to be afraid, *señor*,' Luis announced as he rejoined the American. '*You* most definitely have!'

Bannock shrugged. Being under threat was nothing new. 'So what would you have me do?'

'Hide!'

'And what about these good people?' Bannock asked, with just a hint of sarcasm, as he gestured around. 'Won't they give me away?'

The younger man frowned, as though insulted by such a question. 'You are my guest, and so under my protection. I will see to it that you are not spoken of. Follow me, *por favor*.'

The soldiers, aware that they were being watched, had deliberately stepped up their pace to a swaggering march, and were now audible inside the walls. Without further comment, Bannock followed Luis back to his room, where he watched in surprise as a rug was pulled back to reveal a sturdy trapdoor.

Lifting it, the Mexican remarked, 'The good fathers who were here before us also had things to hide. You will be safe down there.'

'What about my weapons?' his guest demanded. 'They'll be a dead giveaway.'

'Already down there,' Luis replied. 'I don't like guns.'

Cautiously descending the stepladder, Bannock retorted, 'Happen you may have need of them *again*, afore long!'

Then the trapdoor closed above him, and he was left in total darkness.

Luis's heart sank as he scrutinized the mounted officers from beneath his wide-brimmed hat. The obvious leader had the look of a strutting peacock, and that kind was always the worst. Standing with the other menfolk, the peon kept his head bowed, eyes down, as the *coronel* dismounted in from of them.

'You will have food prepared immediately,' Vallejo

snapped at the quite rightly subservient villagers. 'And you can count yourselves fortunate that we are only here for the night.'

Without awaiting a response, he then strolled proprietorially through the entranceway and on into the mission compound. He was surprised at the amount of space. There would be enough room to bivouac all his men within San Marcos' crumbling walls. Their comfort was of little concern to him, but to have them all in one place limited the opportunities for desertion. Not that there was really anywhere to go!

Capitan Ugalde watched for a moment as his commanding officer began an inspection of the living quarters. He well knew that such a man would be concerned only with finding the most comfortable billet, whilst leaving all military duties to his subordinates. Around him, the nervous inhabitants were rapidly stoking fires and preparing food. The burden of feeding such a body of soldiers could well leave them without any for themselves, but that might be the least of their worries. He beckoned to a hulking *sargento* standing nearby. Protocol meant that Ugalde would normally have passed instructions on to the individual company *tenientes*, but he had good reason for bypassing that in this instance.

'Montoya. These simple people are our fellow countrymen, who have given us no trouble. We are here for food and a place to rest, and *nothing* more. Do I make myself clear?'

The massive, pockmarked non-com grinned at him. Or it might have been a scowl. It was difficult to tell with features such as his. Montoya was a veteran of numerous campaigns, including the ill-fated one against the Texicans. Rumour had it that he had received the great scar on his right cheek during the final assault on the Alamo Mission at San Antonio de Bexar. It was common knowledge that his own men were terrified of him, but there was no denying that he was invaluable in a fight. Unfortunately he had a fondness for rape and pillage that wasn't shared by Captain Ugalde.

'*Sí, mi capitan.* All I want is to fill my belly and sleep,' the bull-necked *sargento* quietly affirmed – and yet something about his expression gave the officer no comfort at all.

Unfortunately, Ugalde knew full well that with two hundred and fifty men scattered about the compound, he had no hope of watching them all. . . especially once darkness had fallen!

CHAPTER SIX

Bannock jerked awake, his eyes searching the inky blackness. Something had obviously disturbed him, but he was unable to discern just what that might be. It all seemed as quiet as dust in a church. His host had very considerately placed a straw mattress in the cellar, or whatever the space was that he was occupying, and so with a full belly the American had soon drifted off to sleep. Amazingly, considering how stuffy the air was, it had been deep and untroubled, and would doubtless have lasted longer.

Then he heard it. The low moan of someone deeply distressed. That was followed by a louder, animal-like snarl, which clearly came from the room above. It was obvious that some dark deed was taking place, and all his instincts warned him to stay put, and even go back to sleep. Unfortunately, Bannock had always been an awkward and curious cuss, not much given to doing the right thing.

Peering around, he searched for his firearms, but they might just as well have been invisible. Not that it would make any sense to use them, with half the Mexican army camped above him. If it came to killing, he would just have to rely on the Bowie knife attached to his belt. The use of cold steel did not come naturally to a lot of white folks, but he had never been afflicted by such niceties.

Easing off the mattress, he found the stepladder by touch. Another, louder moan reached him, and he decided that it had to be from a female. Pepita's lovely features suddenly swam into his mind, and with his pulse beginning to race, he prayed that it wasn't her who was being abused. Placing the blade of the massive knife between tightly clenched teeth, Bannock cautiously began climbing. Almost immediately, his head gently butted up against the trapdoor. With beads of sweat forming on his brow, he recognized that this was the point of no return. Once he raised the door, he was committed. *Or* he could just return to the ground, and meekly wait until Luis came for him. If that man was ever able to!

'Oh, the hell with it!' he decided. His intervention had never really been in doubt, because the smell of death seemed to follow some men around, and so it was with him.

Recalling how solid the trapdoor was, the American ascended another step and then put his shoulders to it. Praying fervently that the hinges wouldn't squeak and give him away, he slowly heaved upwards. Ignoring the sudden pain in his side, he kept up the pressure until the rug fell away. The frenzied noises in the room were abruptly louder and more immediate. Barely daring to breath, Bannock peered over at the cot where he had spent most of the last three days. The flickering light, provided by a single foul-smelling tallow candle, served only to emphasize the disagreeable sight before him.

A brutal act of rape was taking place, which sadly did not really surprise him. With soldiers in the settlement, he had suspected something of the sort. It was the degree of violence involved that sickened him. A huge bear of a man, wearing filthy Long Johns, had pinioned his victim to the cot. The helpless woman's skirt had ridden up around her waist, as the great brute pounded away inside her. Both his hands gripped her by the throat, as though he was throttling the life out of her. Even in the poor light, Bannock could see fresh blood on both her clothes and the blanket, and he was pretty damn sure that it didn't belong to the vicious assailant.

Whilst knowing that he had to act fast, the American also recognized that there could be no half measures. In his weakened condition, and up against such a monster of a man, the only course of action was to kill, and kill quickly.

The ghastly sexual activities on the cot meant that the couple were oblivious to anything else, and so Bannock remained unnoticed as he eased up into the room. After carefully settling the trapdoor on to the floor, he remained in a crouching position and took hold of the huge knife in his right hand. The bovine rapist continued to grunt with effort, but his victim was apparently no longer able to offer any resistance. It was going to be touch and go even to save her life, but her potential saviour knew that he had to get the timing just right.

Drawing in a deep breath, Bannock watched as the *soldado* abruptly arched his head back in apparent ecstasy, and recognized that this was the best chance that he'd get. Surging forwards like a great cat, he seized a mat of greasy hair with his left hand, and thrust the Bowie's great blade into his victim's throat. Not content with that, he then twisted the knife for good measure. A geyser of blood flowed over the poor woman, and it was as well that she was still unable to scream.

The huge soldier's dead weight collapsed forwards on to his former victim, his hands still around her throat, but no longer squeezing. Extracting his knife, Bannock swiftly wiped it clean on the Long Johns, before sheathing it. Then, after carefully gauging the distance, he grabbed hold of the corpse's shoulders and heaved with all his might. The now lifeless body toppled off the cot and over to the open trapdoor. With gravity taking over, its massive bulk crashed down into the cellar, to end up in a bloody heap at the bottom of the steps.

For the first time the distraught female was able to breathe properly, but Bannock couldn't allow her to vent her desperate emotion: crouching next to the cot, he gently placed a hand over her mouth and put a finger to his lips. Although coated in blood, she stared into his eyes, and slowly nodded her assent. Although undoubtedly traumatized, the woman had sense enough to realize that she was still in mortal danger.

Knowing that they could be discovered at any time, Bannock pointed to the trapdoor. Gesturing that he would return below, he indicated that she should then close it, and pull the rug back into place. Thankfully, she was both quick on the uptake and resourceful. Sliding off the bed, she removed the bloodied blanket and rapidly wiped herself down with it. Then she rolled it into a ball and tossed it after her attacker. His discarded uniform went the same way. Her rescuer nodded with satisfaction, and made for the stepladder. The woman still had an awful lot of blood on her, but doubtless she would be able to find somewhere to wash it off.

As he carefully retreated down the steps, Bannock glanced back up at the female he had saved. Such a description did beg the question, *was* she really safe? All she could do was try to remain in hiding until the soldiers moved on. If they did. He favoured her with an understanding smile, but had no advice to offer. He had already done all that he could. Even in the dim light, he could see the anxiety on her features that was only partially masked by blood. Then, somehow, she managed to return the gesture. Momentarily her face lit up, and it suddenly occurred to him that there might be a pretty woman under all the gore, which would, of course, explain why she had been selected. Then he was back down into the pit, only this time he had to share it with a monstrous corpse.

With the trapdoor slowly dropping into place, he just had time to clamber over Montoya's body and back on to the straw mattress. Most people would have found it difficult to settle in such circumstances, but Bannock was no stranger to violent death, and he had never yet been harmed by a cadaver. And so, as his heart rate began to return to normal, the reluctant assassin gradually began to drift off to sleep again. Vaguely he wondered just what the morning would bring, and then he was gone.

As natural light flooded into the cellar, its only living occupant jerked awake. It was as though only a moment had passed, and yet he was rubbing his eyes after another refreshing sleep. Then he turned, saw the blood-soaked corpse and grimaced. There had to be better sights to wake up to. Like maybe the young lady that he'd assisted. However one looked at it, it had been quite a night!

'You are unhurt, *señor*?' Luis's anxious features appeared above him.

Bannock grunted. 'You asking me, or this piece of shit?' Then he smiled to take the sting out of it. 'Yeah, yeah, just funning. I'm OK, I guess. My side's sore, an' I'm starving, but I'm alive. What about the girl?'

The *girl* suddenly appeared next to his host. Her features were now cleaned of the victim's blood, and she was beaming from ear to ear.

'*Gracias, gracias,*' she gushed, time after time, until finally Luis had to gently move her aside. It occurred to the American that cleaned up, she was more than just pretty: she was gorgeous. He understood immediately why she had been singled out by the predatory non-com.

'Come up from there, *por favor,*' Luis implored. 'The *soldados* have gone, and you must eat.'

'Sounds good to me,' Bannock responded. 'But first you need to drop a rope down here. This big bastard'll be starting to stiffen, an' soon you'll never get him through the hatch.'

'*Sí, sí.* We will do all that. You must follow Ana to the fire. We have a little food hidden away for the hero.'

'Hero?' replied Bannock quizzically. 'Why, what have I done?'

As he clambered up into the room, Ana, petite and dark-haired, planted a kiss on his forehead, before seizing his arm and leading him to the compound. He was quite unprepared for what awaited him. Whereas before the villagers had been nervous and suspicious of him, now they were smiling broadly and keen to catch his eye. Some even patted him gently on his back as he passed by.

Ana led him over to a fire where Pepita was waiting. It was obvious that the youngster was to act as translator. And boy, could she talk. At first, Bannock listened attentively to her rendition of Ana's voluble thanks, but finally he could resist the food smells no longer. With eyes wide, he pointed plaintively at his mouth, and everyone laughed.

It was as he was happily feeding, watched by a beaming audience, that Luis and two other men dragged the *soldado*'s corpse into the open. They were sweating from the effort, and once there it was obvious that they were at a loss as to what to do with it. Their glances kept drifting hopefully over to the American. Many of the villagers, all of whom were seeing the cadaver for the first time, gasped in shock at the gory mess on display.

'So it's not enough that I kilt the bastard,' that man remarked through a mouthful of beans. 'Now you want me to tell you what to do with the body!'

Luis shrugged expressively. 'We are simple people, *señor*. Unused to the ways of war.'

'Huh,' Bannock grunted non-committedly. 'Tell me this. When those soldier boys pulled out of here, did they know he'd gone missing?'

Luis pondered on that for a moment. 'It did not seem so. They moved out just after dawn, once the *coronel* decided we had no more food. Or so he thought. He didn't realize that we had moved our cattle further down the arroyo while they were still marching in here. We had even managed to hide away a few of our chickens. His kind are all the same. He was just a *cerdo*! How you say? Pig!'

The *coronel*'s parentage was of no interest to the American. He had already decided what needed to be done with the rapist . . . *if* these self-proclaimed simple people had the *cojones* for it. 'OK, listen up. You need to strip him of those Long Johns and tie him over a donkey. Believe me, I don't envy you that. Then take him in the same direction that his friends went and dump him in the open. Scatter all his clothes nearby.'

Luis was the only adult to comprehend all this, and his horrified reaction was understandable. 'But for why, *señor*?'

Bannock sighed. It was like dealing with children. 'Because if his *compadres* come back looking for him, it'll seem like he deserted and got himself caught by some horse Indians. Only problem is, he looks too damn good for that right now. The son of a bitch needs a bit more work.'

Understanding and confusion were alternating on the Mexican's features at a notable rate. 'In what way?' he tentatively asked.

Another sigh. 'Mealtimes don't last long around here, do they?' Swallowing another mouthful, Bannock got to his feet and unsheathed his Bowie knife. Ambling over to the prone corpse, he awkwardly knelt down and suddenly plunged the blade into the unresisting torso. After repeating the action many times, he then seized the non-com's hair and neatly sliced through the scalp until the whole gory mess came away in his hand.

Women and children cried out in shock, and Luis displayed genuine anger. 'There was no need for such a display in front of them!'

Bannock was completely unrepentant. 'There was every God-damn need! 'Cause he ain't the only bad *hombre* in Sonora. Time'll come when the only way you folks can survive out here is to get mean. Real mean. And the sooner you *all* learn that, the more chance you've got.' He tossed the scalp over towards the other man. 'Here. Keepsake for you.' With that, he returned to the fire and calmly continued eating. He had a lot of catching up to do, and he wasn't sure just when his welcome would wear out.

It was late morning before the young *teniente* summoned sufficient nerve to approach Capitan Ugalde. It wasn't that he was afraid of his senior officer. Far from it, in fact, because the experienced *capitan* was actually considerably more agreeable than most of his kind. No, it was more the fact that he knew that he had let him down, and he was ashamed.

'I am distressed to report that *Sargento* Montoya is missing, *mi capitan.*'

That man stared at his junior with disbelief. He glanced ahead to make sure that Vallejo was out of earshot. 'When did you last see him?'

Even though well tanned, there was no hiding the colour that flooded to the *teniente*'s face. 'I . . . I'm not too sure, sir. His men made no mention of it when we left San Marcos.'

Ugalde grunted expressively. Such a disclosure didn't surprise him in the slightest. What irked him was that this promising young officer had been so easily hoodwinked. 'He is . . . *was* under *your* command, Felipe. It is your job to know where all your men are.'

The other man bowed his head in supplication. 'With your permission, sir, I will go back and search for him. We are not missing any animals, and he could not get far on foot.'

Ugalde thought for a moment, before shaking his head emphatically. 'What if he stole a donkey from the villagers?' Before the young man could reply, he continued with, 'Mostly you are a good officer, Felipe, and I would not wish to lose you as well. So we will both go back . . . once I have obtained permission from our esteemed *coronel.*'

Some little inflection in those last words made the

teniente smile. Neither he nor his peers had any great affection for their haughty commanding officer. They all knew who the real soldier was at their head, and so Felipe had no doubt that Ugalde would get permission. Whether they would see Montoya again was a different matter entirely.

Bannock lounged on a blanket near the open fire, content to watch the comings and goings of the villagers as they went about their various tasks. Many worked in the large cornfield beyond the walls. With constant irrigation required, the toil was endless. Those people in his vicinity appeared to have got over their collective shock at his brutal treatment of the soldier's corpse. After all, apart from being already dead, the man had also been a rapist.

Ana had finally presented her husband, so that through Pepita he, too, could offer his heartfelt thanks. The fact that the highly attractive young woman was married should not have come as a surprise, yet the disclosure was something of a disappointment to the American, because he had been quite taken by the warmth of her gratitude. It also made him wonder just where the hell her spouse had been, when her honour required defending. As the two of them stood before him, their eyes kept drifting nervously to the massive knife on his belt. Smiling, he had unsheathed it and offered it for inspection.

'Tell them they have nothing to fear from such a weapon,' Bannock instructed Pepita. 'It's only as dangerous as the man using it.' As they absorbed the translation, they both bowed graciously, but neither chose to touch it. It reminded him that, in his experience, most people preferred to let others do their killing for them.

The hours passed, and Bannock began to notice people glancing towards the entrance. It, too, occurred to him that the three men were long overdue from such a relatively simple task. It had been their stated intention not to travel too far from the mission. Sighing, he placed the nipple pick that he had been cleaning his fingernails with back into his trousers pocket and slowly got to his feet. Using the need to relieve himself as an excuse, he drifted outside, beyond the disintegrating walls and into the desert where there were no labourers.

Having just completed his ablutions, he suddenly heard footsteps from somewhere behind him in the scrub. Twisting to investigate provoked a sharp twinge in his left side, but not enough to prevent him drawing his knife. What he saw caused his brow to furrow, because it was obvious that a well-considered plan had not necessarily come to fruition.

Luis, alone and on foot, staggered towards him. Blood seeped from a gash on his forehead. As he spotted the American, relief flooded over his open features, but that quickly turned to fear as he glanced back over his shoulder.

'Are they still out there?' the Mexican called out.

'Not a one that I can see, whoever they may be,' Bannock responded. 'But you look like you've done seen a ghost.'

'Devils more like,' Luis gasped haltingly as he joined him. He obviously required rest, but the urge to talk proved stronger. 'We had just dropped that *cerdo* to the ground. They came out of nowhere, howling and screaming. Filled poor Miguel and Pedro with arrows. I let go of the donkey and ran for my life. They must have wanted that creature more than they wanted me, but still I thought I was dead for sure.'

Bannock's eyes were like chips of ice, as he put the inevitable question. 'Comanches?'

Capitan Ugalde saw the carrion birds long before the two officers reached the bodies. The gross creatures flapped about, stabbing and tearing at naked flesh. Despite the heat, he felt a great chill descend over him, because somehow he knew with dreadful certainty that one of the men would be their missing *sargento*. Drawing and cocking his privately purchased Colt revolver, the *capitan* resisted the strong urge to blast away at the birds. The surrounding terrain was uneven, and quite capable of concealing other, far more dangerous predators.

Turning to his ashen-faced subordinate, he ordered, 'Draw your weapon, and keep watch. When we reach them, remain mounted.' There was no response, and so he added in a far harsher tone, 'Answer me, *teniente*!'

Finally, the young man found his voice. '*Lo siento, mi capitan.* I will do as you say.'

Grunting, Ugalde urged his now reluctant horse towards the dreadful scene. As expected, Montoya's bulky figure lay there, the features barely recognizable.

Leaving his horrified *teniente* to retch in the dust, he dismounted and carefully inspected the cadavers. All three had been stripped naked, their clothes casually discarded nearby. Body parts had been removed, and each man had been scalped. He had no doubt that such gruesome slaughter was the work of savages, yet nevertheless the make-up of the three bodies puzzled him. And of course, savages could belong to all nationalities!

The two slightly built Mexicans had apparently been perforated with arrows, which had then been removed for re-use. Their corpses were literally coated with dried blood. *Sargento* Montoya, on the other hand, had had his throat savagely sliced, which appeared to be the cause of death. He, too, had then been scalped and cut about the body, yet there was far less blood around those injuries. It was as though the gratuitous mutilation had occurred some considerable time after death. And yet surely they had all been killed at the same time ... or was it just intended that it should appear that way? Which then begged the question, why had he been with two apparent strangers? There had been no other desertions in the night. Ugalde had confirmed that before leaving the column. And in any case, their clothes were those of simple peons. It just didn't make sense.

Shaking his head, the *capitan* glanced up at his companion. 'Something very strange has taken place here, Felipe. Or maybe somewhere else.'

The young man stared at him uncomprehendingly. This was the first time that he had seen violent death close up, and all he wanted to do was ride like the wind.

Anywhere, just to get away from it. Whatever awaited them in California couldn't possibly be worse than this. But then a peculiar look came to his superior's face, as that man stared off into the middle distance, the dead apparently forgotten.

'It is time for us to report back to the column,' Ugalde abruptly announced, as he swiftly returned to the saddle. 'Keep a steady pace, and stay next to me.'

The *teniente* was both relieved and surprised, and so it was annoying to be suddenly troubled by guilt. 'Shouldn't we perhaps bury Montoya first?' he queried reluctantly.

As he urged his mount into motion, the *capitan* emphatically shook his head. 'If we were to do that, we might just as well dig *five* graves. The fat *bastardo* should have obeyed orders. So he stays where he lies!'

Set-tainte's cruel features displayed both calculation and cunning as he watched the hated Mexican *soldados* ride off to the northwest. He had quite deliberately spared them, despite protests from some of the warriors assembled behind him, because where there were two, so there could very likely be others. Far better to let them learn lessons from the dead, and ride off in peace. That way, he and his followers could loot and pillage softer targets. Like the pitiful residents of the old adobe mission. That settlement promised prisoners aplenty for torture and trade.

Unconsciously he shifted the heavy weight of the captured volleygun across his left thigh. He was aware that possession of such a weapon had added greatly to his prestige, because no one in the war party had ever seen anything remotely like it before. After recovering the Nock from near the wreckage of the massive white man's body, Set-tainte had spent a great deal of time reloading it. The lengthy task had been far from easy, because apart from anything else he could only guess at how much powder to tip down each barrel. He was even prepared to tolerate the antique flintlock mechanism. But now, after carrying it for many miles, he was beginning to wish wholeheartedly that he had left it at their base camp, or even traded it to one of the many warriors who unwittingly admired it. One thing was for sure, though: before he did dispose of it, he would use it against the enemies of his people. And being Comanches, that included pretty much everyone else in the human race!

There was one other thing niggling the war chief, and that was the fact that one of the men accompanying the laden donkey had escaped to spread the alarm. In itself, that wasn't cause for concern, but Set-tainte had seen the condition of the original butchered corpse, and it had given him pause. Who was he? Why had he needed to die, and why go to so much trouble disposing of him? Such brutal handiwork was not likely to be the product of a simple peon. Whoever had done that was a born killer, just like the Comanches themselves!

CHAPTER SEVEN

Luis sat on the cot that Bannock had inhabited for the first few days of his stay in San Marcos. Next to him was Pepita, an arm tightly linked in his. Since her father's return, bloodied and shaken, she had not moved from his side. The American sat on a chair opposite, his Colt revolvers now conspicuously back in his belt. It was very obvious to him that the Mexican had a great deal on his mind, and that at least some of it involved his guest.

'Could they have been the same Comanches that attacked you?' Luis asked.

Bannock nodded. 'Seems kind of likely. They've travelled a mighty long way from Comancheria. Makes sense to get their fill of raiding before they head back, and there's nothing they like better than doing that in Mexico. Kind of makes you wish those soldier boys were still around, don't it?'

Luis sighed, and clutched his daughter all the harder. It was obvious that his terrifying brush with the Indians was still etched into his mind. 'How can we hope to fight them, *señor*?'

Bannock's eyes narrowed. 'Maybe you folks should have thought of that before you settled out here ... with your children an' all. The Comanches have had free rein over northern Mexico for decades.'

A certain fire seemed to ignite in the other man's eyes. 'Perhaps you don't know what it is to be poor, *señor*. We have no money, and no government to help us, so we had to settle on land that no one else wanted.'

'Except that now, others hanker after what you've brought to it,' Bannock retorted sharply, apparently unmoved by their predicament. He, too, knew what it was to be broke, but it wasn't his way to comment on such things. His credo had always been, 'never complain, and never explain'. But then, completely unexpectedly, the little girl with the red bonnet suddenly loomed large in his memory. Raw emotion registered on his tough features, and his eyes grew damp. 'It's no different in the US of A, you know. Poor folks, or those running from something, have to move out west to get free land, but then they butt up against the horse Indians, and not all of them make it.'

'*You* could help us fight them, Señor Bannock,' Luis remarked hopefully.

The American grunted. So that was why he had been invited to join the two of them. He shook his head emphatically. 'Nah, I reckon not. I've helped you, an' you've helped me. So let's call it evens, and forget that you people have probably come out ahead. Sell me a burro, and I'll be on my way.'

Luis's disappointment was plain to see, but it was nothing compared to that of Pepita. Releasing her father, she ran crying over to the startled American and began to beat on his chest with her little fists. 'You saved me. I thought we were friends,' she yelled bitterly.

Completely taken aback, he did not even try to resist. Uppermost in his mind was one thought. 'Why does she have to be dressed in red?'

Embarrassed, Luis came over to stop her, but Bannock waved him away. Then, gently taking her wrists, he looked into the little girl's tear-stained eyes. 'I'll make a deal with you,' he stated softly. 'If you stop beating on me, I'll stay another night and think over what your pa has said. What do you say to that?'

Pepita stared at him, her tear-stained eyes wide as saucers. Gradually, with a lot of sniffing and swallowing, she calmed down enough to nod once.

Bannock's rough-hewn features crinkled into a smile. 'Well, good for you,' he replied warmly, before adding softly to her father. 'Let's hope it turns out to be quieter than last night, huh?'

Unbeknown to Luis, those words were said in genuine hope, but without any real expectation, because unlike the villagers, Bannock had a pretty fair idea of what was coming!

As the two officers rejoined the slow-moving column, *Coronel* Vallejo gratefully called a halt. In truth, even though well mounted, he had had enough of the interminable slog for one day. California's governor would just have to wait that bit longer. He was genuinely glad to have the experienced *capitan* back, because if anyone had the temerity to attack them, he was not sure just how he would react. Not that he intended to show his relief. Pride had too strong a hold over him.

'What of the *sargento*?' he enquired somewhat coldly. 'Had he decided to raise goats with the villagers?'

'Far from it,' Ugalde replied. 'In fact I believe it was someone in San Marcos who murdered him.'

The *coronel* was taken aback. 'Montoya dead! That is very unfortunate. So I take it that you did find him, then.'

'What was left of him, *sí*. Along with two peons killed by Indians. Probably Comanches.'

'How do you know it was Indians?' Vallejo asked somewhat naively.

'Nobody else butchers a man like they do,' retorted Ugalde, rather more harshly than he had intended. He was observing his superior closely, because he had more to say, but wasn't quite sure how to proceed. He was aware of the young *teniente* at his side looking totally nonplussed. Vallejo obviously sensed that there was more to come, because he looked at the *capitan* expectantly.

'And those same heathens were watching us all the time,' Ugalde finally divulged.

'Did you actually see them?' Vallejo demanded.

The other man shook his head. 'I didn't need to. I could sense them all around us.'

Whilst young Felipe was horrified with his apparent brush with death, their commander wasn't quite sure how to react to such a statement. Someone of his ilk had little tolerance for so-called 'sixth sense'.

'I believe we were *allowed* to leave, because the

Comanches had other plans,' Ugalde doggedly continued. 'That can only mean that they intend to attack San Marcos.'

Vallejo studied his subordinate closely. He was becoming increasingly irritated by the lack of substance in the report, and he especially didn't like where it was leading. 'And?'

'They are citizens of Mexico, *mi coronel*,' Ugalde stated somewhat officiously. 'It is our sworn duty to protect them. Therefore I wish to return to San Marcos with the *teniente* and fifty men.'

It was Vallejo's turn to be horrified. 'Absolutely out of the question,' he retorted. 'We have been assigned our mission by the *president* personally. That is the only duty that I recognize, and it surely takes precedence over the uncertain needs of a group of destitute squatters. Besides, by the time you got back there it would be too late. I, too, have heard stories of these Comanches. It is said they are devils on horseback.'

'Nevertheless, I wish to try, *mi coronel*. Whatever happens in California, fifty men won't change the outcome one way or another.'

The two men stared fixedly at each other, neither one prepared to back down. Vallejo possessed the rank, Ugalde the field experience. In a moment of prescience, it suddenly occurred to the young *teniente* that the fate of San Marcos and all of its inhabitants quite possibly hung on the outcome!

It was the best of all possible nights for a raid. A huge, luminescent moon hung over a cloudless sky, allowing easy progress over the harsh landscape. The small herd of scrawny cattle beckoned, and Set-tainte nodded with satisfaction. The omens appeared to be good, and if all went well, the next action would be a full-scale murder raid on the isolated settlement. The prospect was so pleasurable that he could almost taste it. And of course a good outcome would also surely enhance his status in the tribe.

The animals were clustered in an arroyo within sight of San Marcos's walls. His intention was to sweep in at speed, slaughter any guards and drive the livestock away. Glancing around at his sparsely glad warriors, the chief bared his teeth with savage glee. Contrary to the inaccurate perceptions of many of the white eyes, these particular Indians were not decked out with feathered headdresses and elaborate war paint. They preferred to travel light and concentrate on what they were best at: warfare in all its glory. This was what they had all been born to, and now yet again it was time.

Lifting the heavy Nock above his head, Set-tainte unleashed a great howl and urged his pony forwards. Screaming like banshees, his men spread out along his flanks, so they advanced in a wide crescent that enveloped the arroyo. A single bleary-eyed guard, Alfredo by name, stared in stupefied shock at the mass of horsemen charging towards him out of the gloom. Even though he'd heard Luis's frightening story, he still hadn't really accepted that he, too, might end up in harm's way. And yet now, unbelievably, the savages were almost upon him!

The sudden commotion spooked the cattle. With

walls on their left and a sizeable stream flowing on their right, they began to flee in exactly the direction intended. The shocking realization that the whole herd would be lost, energized the normally placid Alfredo, and he drew from his belt the only weapon that he possessed. Swinging the razor-sharp machete at the nearest rider, he managed, more by luck than judgement, to strike the Comanche's left thigh. The blade sliced deep, right to the bone, eliciting a howl of agony from his victim. With blood gushing from his leg, that man lost control of his pony, and the animal veered off away from the main band towards the adobe walls.

Surprised and exhilarated by his own apparently deadly skill, Alfredo turned to shout his defiance at the rest of the warriors. But before any words had even left his mouth, an arrow struck him just above the bridge of his nose, penetrating his skull and driving on into his brain. Death was gory but instantaneous, which in a way was a blessing, because had he been captured his fate would have been unimaginable.

As the solitary night guard toppled backwards into the dust, the terrified cattle gathered speed and disappeared into the night, followed closely by their new owners. The sole exception was Set-tainte, who briefly reined in within sight of San Marcos's walls. He watched angrily as his wounded compatriot collapsed sideways from his pony, and lay moaning and twitching on the ground.

It occurred to the chief that he should at least attempt a recovery of the animal, but then flickering lights appeared within the settlement, and he recognized that such an attempt would be too risky on his own. As he turned away to rejoin the others, his lean features were transformed into a wolfish smile. Even if the Mexicans caught the pony, they would get little use from it, because in a very short time, he and his warriors were coming back. And then these pathetic farmers would learn just what it meant to encounter a Comanche war party!

'Seems as though it's a life for a life,' Bannock commented quietly, as he gazed down at the suffering Comanche. 'Well, at least they know one of you fellas had some fight in him.'

'But this one is still alive, *señor*.' Luis commented innocently.

The two men were with a number of other light sleepers, congregated just beyond the walls. One of the villagers had taken hold of the pony's reins and was leading it away. The others were gazing glumly over at the now deserted arroyo. One pony seemed a poor exchange for a herd of cattle.

Bannock grunted. 'Looking at that leg, he's likely gonna bleed out before we finish this conversation. And if he doesn't, then so much the worse for him. What was your night hawk called?'

'Alfredo,' Luis replied sadly. 'He was a brave *hombre*.'

'The question is, are the rest of you prepared to fight like he did? Because after tonight, there ain't any doubt in my mind that those bastards will be back. And next time it'll be a murder raid!'

A mixture of fear and determination came to the Mexican's eyes. 'To protect our families, we will have to fight, but can we hope to survive without help?'

Bannock chuckled dryly. 'I reckon not. That's why I've decided to stick around for a while longer. Hell, it ain't as though I've got anywhere else to be, right now.'

His eyes welling up with tears, Luis clasped the other man's hands, but the American hadn't finished. 'Besides, seems like I just can't get away from the killing. Hand me that machete.' Hefting the deadly implement in his hand, he remarked, 'Appears like this here's the only weapon you've got in this place that's worth a damn.' So saying, he strode over to the dying Comanche.

The warrior, his face contorted with pain, still managed to stare up at him with venom in his eyes.

'I ain't gonna try and make you plead for your miserable hide,' Bannock announced. 'Because I know just how tough you cockchafers are. So all I'll say to you is, rot in hell!'

With that, he took a mighty swing that was pretty much guaranteed to hurt his injured side. When force was combined with skill, the heavy blade wasn't just effective against limbs: it could also cleave through the neck of a grown man, which is exactly what happened. With Luis and the others looking on in horror and disgust, the Comanche's head was cleanly separated from its torso. As a torrent of blood gushed forth, the hideous trophy rolled a few inches before settling in the dust, a now lifeless gaze seemingly aimed accusingly at his killer.

Ignoring the pain from his wound, Bannock casually tossed the machete to the ground, and then fixed hard eyes on his host. 'Afore you get to bleating, I did that for a reason. I want that bastard's head on a spike over the main gate. It'll show the war party that our intentions are serious, and it might just goad them into making a mistake.' He waited a moment for that to sink in before adding, 'Come first light, we're gonna have to see about how to defend this place, so I'm heading for some more shuteye.'

As he turned away, the startled peon called after him. 'If all *Americanos* are like you, God help us if our two countries ever go to war.'

CHAPTER EIGHT

Even as the new day dawned, word had already spread that the mysterious *gringo* intended to help them in their fight against the raiders from the north. After the death of their friend Alfredo, no one could doubt that the settlement would be next. Yet as the villagers stepped out into the compound and discovered the grisly severed head on display, some of them began to wonder who they should be most afraid of.

Unusually for the sociable Mexicans, the communal breakfast turned out to be a hurried and uncomfortable repast. Not only was Bannock wearing his fearsome knife and brace of Colts, but he had also produced two long guns. Having placed these meaningfully against a wall, the American began thoughtfully pacing the compound, apparently scrutinizing the meagre defences. In truth, he already knew what had to be done, but it didn't hurt to put on a show. And his inspection did confirm his earlier opinion that the former church, as the strongest building, would have to act as a last ditch defensive position if such were necessary. But it would serve no good purpose to mention any of that just yet.

Once Luis and his daughter appeared, it was time to take the bull by the horns, but first that man had his own suggestion to make. 'Shouldn't we try and build some of these walls up, and get the gates back on?' he asked uncertainly.

'It's too damn late for any of that, mister,' retorted Bannock uncompromisingly. 'They're gonna be down your throats before you know it. Besides, Comanches don't like high walls and enclosed spaces, and if they chose *not* to make a frontal attack, it could turn out even worse for you.'

Luis was mystified, and as Pepita helped with the translation, so were the others. 'How could that be?' he enquired.

Bannock shook his head despairingly. 'You fellas really don't know what you're up against, do you? Think about it. Since you haven't got around to digging a well, your only water supply is the river over yonder, which is fine *until* somebody gets between you and it. All they have to do is surround this place and lob in a few fire arrows, and suddenly you're in deep shit. These buildings might be adobe, but they're still vulnerable. The roof supports are all wood, and I'm betting that there's brushwood across them under the bricks.' The American briefly paused for breath. He really couldn't remember a time when he'd had to do so much damn jawing.

'So the best and *only* chance you've got is to encourage them to ride on in,' he continued. 'And then hit them hard. And keep on hitting. Most always,

Comanches don't like taking heavy casualties. Makes them think the spirits are against them. That head ain't up there on a spike just for the hell of it. No siree. It's to get them riled up and angry, and out for blood. That way the sons of bitches are less apt to think straight, which could just give us an edge.'

'So what *do* we do?' Luis asked resignedly.

'For a start, I want men up on the walls, standing guard. Anything moves out there, I need to know about it.'

Such a demand was obviously sensible, and following Luis's translation, two men scurried up on to the highest parts of the walls.

Next, Bannock indicated the main entrance. 'Get what's left of those gates off the hinges and inside. Lean them up against the walls, out of sight. It'll encourage the cockchafers to come in through there. Once they're in, I'll be wanting your men to push them across the opening to block the way out.'

Luis was aghast. As the only English-speaking adult, he was bearing the brunt of Bannock's revelations. '*Madre de Dios*, but that is madness. They'll slaughter us all!'

'Not if we slaughter *them* first,' Bannock retorted. 'Which brings me to long guns. Anybody fired a rifle before?'

The translation was met with a sea of blank faces.

'Jesus H. Christ! Does anyone *want* to fire a rifle?'

This time, one man nodded, pointing tentatively towards the Hawken, rather than the captured musket. There was a guarded gleam in his eyes that hinted at his

97

decision not being entirely random.

'Oh, so you fancy a real gun, do you?' Bannock chuckled. 'Good choice.'

The volunteer's name was Tomas, and he had obviously used some kind of rifle before, because he tucked the butt into his shoulder and glanced down the long barrel with every appearance of competence.

'I'll have to take him on trust,' the American remarked. 'We can't risk any practice shots. I don't want those God-damned dirt worshippers knowing that they're up against firearms until it's too late for them to back off. It's something else that might give us an edge.' After Luis had translated, he added, 'What about this musket? Are you game?'

The Mexican glanced at his daughter before nodding. '*Sí señor.* After all, I am fighting for her life.'

'Damn right you are,' the other man retorted. 'Now, what other weapons are there in this place? Both of you ask them. Quickly now. There ain't no knowing how long we've got.'

Under the joint urging of father and daughter, the villagers produced a mixture of machetes and pitchforks, and one double-barrelled shotgun. That at least had some potential.

'Is there a blacksmith or metal-worker who can saw a length off the barrels?' Bannock demanded.

'*Sí, sí.* I can do,' responded an elderly man eagerly.

It seemed that the peons were finally being infused by their visitor's sense of urgency, and his next demand intrigued them. Prowling around the compound like a caged beast, he shouted, 'Any kind of netting, or coils of rope?'

It transpired that there was none of the former, but plenty of the latter. 'Lay it on the ground from side to side in front of the entrance. Two strong men on each end. Use it to trip the ponies. A Comanche on foot is apt to be more reasonable.'

His two translators were struggling to keep pace, but he ploughed on anyway. 'Think on this. When they ride in here, we'll *all* be fighting for our lives. And if we lose, then your women and children lose as well. Savvy?'

Such talk definitely hit a collective nerve, and they all stared at him, entranced. And still he hadn't finished. 'But all this just ain't enough to get the drop on a big war party. We need something to really give them pause. I need a container made of wood. Something that we can fill with stones and any small bits of metal you can turn up.'

Not for the first time that day, Luis was completely baffled. '*Por que, señor?*'

On this occasion, the lean *gringo* didn't say a word. Instead, he produced a large powder flask from his jacket and winked broadly at the assembled villagers before turning away towards the nearest cooking fire. They perhaps thought that he was about to provide them with a demonstration, but far from it. He had given them all plenty to think about, and suddenly felt unaccountably hungry. Perhaps the prospect of bloody violence had honed his appetite. Grabbing a bowl, he spooned out a large helping of the ubiquitous beans, and proceeded to wolf them down.

All around him there was a hive of activity, as the

inhabitants of San Marcos came to terms with the very real prospect that they could soon be fighting for their lives. And yet it wasn't long before they began to realize that waiting could be an ordeal in itself!

Much later that afternoon, Set-tainte listened to his scout's report with a mixture of outrage and astonishment. That their seriously wounded comrade had died, came as no surprise. But that his severed head was now displayed above the settlement was something else again. No one could be allowed to treat a Comanche warrior in such a fashion.

As he raged and cursed at the cloudless sky above, one very definite thought clearly emanated from the seething maelstrom of his mind. If these pathetic farmers were trying to provoke him, then they had succeeded! They needed to learn fear and respect. The chief had intended to take his large war party in a rapid sweep around the walls, to emphasize their overwhelming strength, but not now. Now he would lead them straight through the main entrance, under the grisly remains and on to slaughter everyone they found.

For some minutes he allowed word of the Mexicans' behaviour to spread amongst his warriors, and then, as anger swelled in their ranks, he motioned them on towards San Marcos. Trailing a cloud of dust, the whole barbaric horde surged forwards. That they would triumph was undoubted, and such knowledge even lessened their habitual fear of enclosed spaces. Because when the inevitable massacre was over, it would be they who controlled that particular space!

*

'*Madre de Dios!*' His voice was strident, fear dripping from every syllable, as the lookout pointed off into the distance.

Ignoring the pain from his partially healed wound, Bannock leapt to his feet and ran for the wall, closely followed by Luis. What he saw came as no surprise. Possibly as many as one hundred riders were approaching at speed. The sight was enough to chill the blood of even the most experienced Indian fighter. What he had been warning everyone about had finally come to pass. The agonizing wait was over, but what was likely to follow would be far worse.

'Women and children out of sight!' the American bellowed. 'The rest of you to your positions. And remember: don't get scared, get angry. This is *your* home!'

As Luis rattled out the translation, all the while gesturing for Pepita to move indoors, Bannock drew his Colts. It wasn't that they were needed just yet, but he knew that many eyes were on him. The simple villagers *needed* to know that he was with them.

As the Comanches rapidly closed in, Bannock waited to see if they would spread out and reconnoitre. A feral grin spread over his face as he realized that they were all heading for the main entrance. The front runners were glaring up at the severed head. His ploy had worked.

'Tell them to be ready near the gates, but to stay out of sight,' he hissed. 'And then find your own spot.'

'But where, *señor*?' Even though armed with both musket and machete, Luis was plainly nervous.

Bannock winked encouragingly. 'So stick with me. But keep that damned toad stabber out of my face.'

Together they returned to the compound. The sound of a great many unshod hoofs grew closer and closer. It was time. Removing one of his precious Lucifers from a pocket, the American knelt down next to an ornate polished wooden box that one of the women had produced. It was a treasured family heirloom, but one that she had been prepared to sacrifice for the greater good. A diminutive hole had been drilled through the side, to allow a short trail of black powder to be laid. That propellant's incendiary properties could be notably unpredictable, and the margin for error was desperately small.

As the Lucifer flared into life, Bannock touched it to the powder. 'Run like hell!' he barked at Luis, and together the two men leapt behind a pile of rubble reclaimed from a disintegrating wall.

After what had seemed a lifetime of waiting, everything suddenly happened at once. The irreconcilably hostile horsemen burst forth into the compound. Because their whole system of warfare was based on rapid movement, they continued to do just that. Without slowing, and with remarkable skill, the leaders flowed out to the sides, searching for victims. This allowed the following warriors to pack in behind them, unwittingly doing exactly as Bannock had anticipated.

With divine timing, the powder charge exploded with a tremendous roar, sending a lethal mixture of wooden splinters and stone and metal fragments in all directions. The Comanches, lightly clad and caught completely unawares, had no defence against the scything objects. Their small buffalo-hide war shields might as well have not existed. And it was the later arrivals, closest to the blast, which suffered most in the carnage. Ponies and their riders endured every conceivable injury. Tender flesh was sliced open or skewered, and bones shattered. As blood flowed from their bronzed bodies, a great cloud of acrid smoke enveloped Bannock's victims.

The cries of distress attested to the success of his plan – and yet the fight had only just begun, because the Comanche leader was quite obviously still alive. Bannock came to that conclusion with a jarring shock, when he suddenly spotted an Indian holding Chet Butler's prized volleygun. Only someone of superior status would have secured that weapon. Which meant it was also very likely that this same war party had participated in his killing, along with the self-styled 'Children of God', and therefore the American had even more reason to seek their destruction.

Bellowing out over the mayhem, he commanded, 'Get those God-damn gates shut!' To ensure that he was understood, Luis swiftly relayed the instructions in strident Spanish.

Seemingly jolted out of a dazed stupor, the villagers assigned to the task appeared from cover, put their shoulders to the weathered timber and heaved. Before the startled marauders could react, the disused gates slid together across the gap, effectively barring their escape. This was the time to throw everything at the Comanches, whilst they were disorientated and hurting . . . and before they could begin to retaliate!

'Now the rope!' Bannock yelled. 'Trip the ponies!' He glanced at Luis. 'What the hell is rope in Mex?'

'*Cuerda*!' that man replied.

'*Cuerda, cuerda*!' the American took up the cry, to be rapidly joined by his interpreter.

Those villagers assigned to that task abruptly appeared, pulling taut on two great lengths of rope. To Bannock, it seemed as though no one could do anything on their own initiative. But then, to be fair, it was unlikely that anyone had been in a battle before.

Although the two lines were dragged along the ground from different starting points, they didn't actually manage to bring many animals down, but a number of riders were unseated and it all kept up the pressure on the beleaguered warriors. Then an arrow tore into the side of one of the men holding an end of rope. The sight of one of their friends writhing on the ground in bloody agony was enough to unnerve the remainder, and they broke and ran for cover.

With only Comanches out in the open, it was time to utilize every weapon that the settlement possessed. 'Pile it into them!' Bannock hollered. 'Slash the ponies. Fight for your lives!' He had no idea whether the rapid translation was accurate, but Luis certainly appeared to be giving it his all!

A warrior by the name of Alaki stared at their voluble opponents in disbelief. Then, urging his mount over to Set-tainte, he yelled, 'It is him. The one who killed all our brothers in the pursuit!'

The startled chief followed his subordinate's glance. It was true that one of the men was no Mexican. 'You are sure?' he demanded.

Then the gunfire started around them, and any reply was lost in the mayhem. An old, grizzled peon leapt out of a doorway, showing great agility for his years, and levelled a wicked-looking sawn-off shotgun at the milling horsemen. He squeezed both triggers in rapid succession, unleashing two deadly discharges of jagged metal. Almost simultaneously, from a nearby window, there came the sharp crack of a .50-calibre Hawken. Three more raiders toppled from their animals, bloodied and twitching their death throes. On the other side of the compound, a double-shotted musket crashed out. In such a mêlée, accuracy was irrelevant. All that counted was the blasting of hot lead into the enemy.

Those battered warriors who had felt the dreadful effects of the explosion but had survived it, were galloping aimlessly around the compound, desperately searching for a way out. The unexpected gunfire only exacerbated their trepidation. Enclosed spaces made them nervous at any time, and now they wanted nothing more to do with San Marcos. Set-tainte realized that if he didn't act fast, their fear would rapidly affect the others.

Raising the distinctive volleygun above his head, the chief shouted out, 'Are you all women or warriors? These Mexican curs have done their worst, and now they are nothing. They have no more power. Kill them all, and take everything!'

105

His warriors heard the familiar voice, and the savage entreaties began to take effect. Instead of thinking only of escape, some of them began to search for enemies to kill. Bannock, too, could sense that this was the tipping point, when the ferocious confrontation could go either way. It was time for him to risk everything.

Drawing in a deep breath, the American rose up from behind cover and strode brazenly into the open. As so often in dire circumstances, calmness settled over him like a cloak. Squaring his shoulders, he glanced around, displaying every appearance of complete scorn for the rampaging Comanches. In each hand he held a cocked revolver, the retractable triggers down and ready.

Recognizing a direct challenge when they saw one, two warriors rode directly for him. One drew back a taut bowstring, whilst the other brandished a hand axe. Others swung around behind him, to cut off any retreat and aid in his destruction. Effectively surrounded by howling enemies, a lesser man would have succumbed to panic . . . and undoubtedly died.

With great deliberation, Bannock squeezed his right forefinger. As the revolver bucked in his hand, the .36 calibre ball smashed into the heavily contorted features of the bowman. With great good fortune, his suddenly uncontrolled arrow skittered off to the side, and buried itself deep into the belly of a pony, unseating its rider.

Even as Bannock raised the barrel to again cock his piece, he simultaneously fired the left-hand Colt. The ball tore into the left breast of the axe-wielding warrior. As the vicious weapon slid from abruptly nerveless fingers, his killer coolly pivoted on his heels to confront those behind him. Again he fired, this time striking a Comanche side on, sending him toppling to the ground.

Like a ferret after its prey, a peon leapt from cover and repeatedly slashed at the wounded Indian with his machete. Encouraged by their ally's quite remarkable lone stand, other Mexicans began to appear around the compound, clutching similar weapons.

Apparently cool and composed, Bannock continued to unleash shot after shot, until he had only one charged chamber remaining in each of his five-chambered Colts. A wide gap had cleared around him, as the warriors now shied away from confronting such a lethal assassin. Seeing so many others shot to hell and dying, any remaining resolve had been shattered. Now, their only intention was flight.

Then Bannock saw the Comanche who held Chet's volleygun attempting to manoeuvre towards him. That 'crowd-pleaser' needed only to be vaguely pointed in his direction, but that was proving to be harder than expected. The heavy weapon demanded two hands, and its new owner's pony was being unintentionally jostled by his own men, in their headlong rush for the nearest low wall.

Levelling his right-hand Colt, Bannock took careful aim at the struggling chief. If he could just drop him, the fight might well be over for good. Carefully he squeezed the trigger, and then cursed volubly. At the very moment of discharge, a warrior had blundered in front of his target. The lead ball struck that luckless individual in the back of his head, spraying warm blood and brain matter over the startled leader.

Sensing someone at his shoulder, Bannock turned to find Luis staring at him, his sallow features alive with excitement. 'Get your people after them,' he ordered. 'Make those bastards wish they'd never set eyes on San Marcos!'

The Mexican grinned wolfishly. He appeared to be enthused by a fire that his guest hadn't seen before. Blood dripped from the blade of his machete, testifying to his newfound aggression.

As more and more villagers pursued the now fleeing Comanches, their leader mopped blood from his eyes, and angrily accepted that, *for the moment*, there was nothing further that he could contribute. Swinging his animal around, he urged it over the nearest adobe barrier and out on to the open ground that suited his people so much better.

Under normal circumstances, such a costly reverse would have sent him and his followers on their way, in search of easier prey. But there was nothing normal about San Marcos, because the former mission contained an individual who appeared to possess a mantel of invincibility, along with a vocation to slaughter every Comanche that he came across. And such a man could not be allowed to live . . . whatever the cost, because the prestige endowed upon his killer would be immense!

CHAPTER NINE

Darkness, such as it was, had fallen, but out there in the gloom many campfires were visible. The Comanches were making no effort to hide their presence. In fact, it seemed almost as though they were attempting to draw the Mexicans out, knowing that in open country they, the well-mounted Indians, were pretty much supreme.

'Is that it? Have we beaten them? Will they leave us alone now?' In the immediate aftermath of the desperate fight, the hopeful questions had come thick and fast through his two translators. Bannock had fervently hoped that they had done enough, but sadly that now appeared not to be the case. Sometimes there was just no accounting for how an Indian would react. Whims and notions strange to a white man meant that they could be very unpredictable.

In an attempt to put a little space between him and the disappointed villagers, the American was now stationed on an undamaged rampart-like section of wall, which boasted a short stretch of walkway behind it. In spite of, or perhaps because of those damn fires, he was very conscious of the nervous glances from the lookout next to him. It was as though the peon was attempting to draw strength from his presence.

Rearranging his grim features in the semblance of a smile, Bannock winked encouragingly and pointed off towards the enemy's encampment. 'Don't look at me. Look at them,' he muttered softly, knowing that he was unlikely to be fully understood.

Sighing, he turned to peer down into the compound. All was quiet, and yet the whole settlement appeared to be out of doors. It was as though, after what they had been through, everyone felt the need for companionship. Because, unlike the strange, embittered Yankee in their midst, they were essentially a social people.

The two dozen or so broken bodies of the fallen Comanches had been dragged into a pile, for disposal at a later time – though it was to be hoped not too much later, because in such a climate they would soon begin to turn. There were no prisoners, or indeed even any ailing survivors within the walls. Bannock had seen to that. He knew full well that a wounded Indian could be even more dangerous than normal, and that hard-learnt knowledge had resulted in a fearful amount of additional bloodletting.

Luis regarded the fearsome *gringo* from under hooded eyelids. He preferred that his observations stayed hidden, because their lethal saviour remained a complete enigma to him. As his daughter stirred in a troubled sleep next to him, he tenderly stroked her hair, but his eyes never left Bannock. Since the one-sided battle, and the gory nightmare of 'attending' to the wounded that had followed, Pepita had clung to him like a limpet. In spite of his strict instructions to stay out of sight, he was painfully aware that she had witnessed far more than anyone her age ever should have.

As the little one again settled, Luis tried to reconcile what he saw. In truth he was somewhat in awe of the frontiersman. The American's personal offensive against the terrible horse warriors had been truly magnificent. In fact, that would make a good name for him: 'The Magnificent One'. It was also apparent that under his gruff exterior he had a good heart. And yet at the same time, he was quite obviously a brutal, ruthless killer who could have no place in any civilized society.

Luis grunted uncomfortably. He was very aware that he, too, had blood on his hands. And although his actions had been justified, they did not sit well with him, because he also recalled the sheer animal blood-lust that had surfaced within him, as he hacked away with his machete. There was also the fact that the *Americano* was only with them because they had asked him to help.

A pitiful wail briefly disturbed the unusual quiet in the settlement. The villager struck by an arrow, whilst attempting to trip the Comanche ponies, was suffering the tortures of the damned. It was unlikely that he would see another sunrise. Luis sighed deeply. All this killing, and for what? Their enemies were still out there, planning God knows what, and his people no longer had access to fresh water.

The fact that that situation was their own fault entirely, never occurred to the Mexican – but he *was* about to discover the raiders' next move.

'Tomas!' Bannock bellowed out in the night. 'Throw me that long gun, pronto.'

The pockmarked peon jerked out of a shallow sleep, his confusion plain to see. The prized Hawken rifle was cradled in his arms, for all the world as though it was his lover. It was certainly a fact that he had come to regard it as his own. Then he heard the thunder of hoofs from beyond the walls, and a glimmer of understanding came to him. The Yankee required his attendance. But then that man yelled his name again and pointed at the weapon with every sign of impatience, and it abruptly dawned on him that it was the rifle alone that was expected. Very grudgingly, Tomas got to his feet and shambled over. Somehow, he now realized, wishful thinking had encouraged him to make an error of judgement, but that didn't make it any easier to take. He had never possessed anything so fine in his life.

'God-damned greaser!' Bannock muttered, barely managing to conceal his intolerance of the Mexican's tardy response. Reaching out, he grabbed the Hawken as it was reluctantly passed up to him, and then checked the seating of the percussion cap.

Out in the gloom, the landscape had suddenly come alive with fast-moving riders apparently carrying burning torches. The lookout next to him stared in horror, as the flickering pools of light rapidly grew closer. It didn't occur to him that the *Americano* might understand exactly what was to come.

'Luis, clear anyone out of those buildings. Now!'

'Even the wounded, *señor*?'

'*Especially* the wounded!' So saying, Bannock levelled his rifle and drew a bead on one of the fast-approaching Comanches. The fact that the warrior was highlighted by the torch of burning brushwood that he carried, only made the sharpshooter's task easier. As his long gun crashed out, the muzzle flash momentarily illuminated the wall, and the target toppled backwards off his mount. Swiftly he began to reload. It would have been quicker to utilize his Colts, but he didn't feel inclined to waste precious powder against fast-moving targets that were unlikely to come in really close. There was another weapon that could maybe do some damage though.

'Get that shotgun up here,' he bawled. Yet even as he spoke, he knew that they had no chance of preventing the majority of the fire arrows and such getting through. As the old-timer with the sawn-off ascended the stairs, various burning projectiles began to rain over the walls. Many fizzled out on adobe bricks, but enough struck timber to get the job done.

As though deliberately taunting their enemies, the Comanches were only targeting the buildings facing the river. It appeared as if they were seeking to entice the foolhardy into making a dash for fresh water with which to fight the fires. As it happened, no one seemed to harbour any such death wish, but the natural instinct to protect their property was leading the Mexicans to make a big mistake. Carrying pots and urns of vital drinking water, many of them rushed towards the spreading flames.

'Let them burn!' Bannock yelled out. From beside him came the comforting roar of the 'two-shoot' gun, as first one barrel and then the second was discharged at the swarming horsemen.

Luis was horrified. 'But *señor*, these are our homes!' he protested from the compound.

The American was unrepentant. 'If you use it on the buildings, what will you drink tomorrow, donkey piss? Remember, those bastards'll likely still be out there!'

As the terrible reality of the situation sank in, the peon stared up at him numbly. Then, after shaking his head, he began to call out to his neighbours. The role of translator was definitely beginning to grate on him. Initially he was greeted with disbelief, as their glances switched between the man they knew so well and the grim-faced stranger up on the wall. Partially illuminated by flickering firelight, Bannock seemed, at that moment, to resemble a vision from hell itself. Only very reluctantly did they put down the various containers and instead concentrate on recovering everything they could from the threatened buildings.

All along one side of the mission compound, on either side of Bannock and his two companions, flames had taken hold. The Comanches had achieved their goal, and had no intention of pressing the attack. With euphoric whoops, they raced back to the safety of their camp. Bannock hadn't quite finished with them, however. He had no intention of allowing them to believe that they could move across the surrounding country with impunity.

Resting his Hawken on the wall before him, he peered down the long barrel and quickly selected a victim. Because of the Indians' habit of greasing their bodies with buffalo fat, myriad bronzed shoulders glistened in the moonlight. A cold smile spread across his features as he settled on one of the front runners. He'd show these cocky sons of bitches! Easing back the first trigger, Bannock held his breath and then gently squeezed the second. Even as his shoulder absorbed the recoil, he knew that he'd got it right. As a warrior slipped sideways off his mount, his executioner just couldn't resist a chuckle.

Tomas stared up at the *Americano* with a mixture of awe and resentment. Was his presence among them a Godsend or a curse? The man was obviously a born assassin, who had undoubtedly saved them earlier that day. But was the violence only continuing because he had aroused the Comanches' wrath? And would they have even attacked in the first place, if he hadn't insisted on displaying the severed head? These difficult issues troubled him, but the time wasn't right to voice them. The brushwood over the supports had caught fire, and now nothing could prevent the roofs from collapsing.

Up on the wall, the heat had grown intense, and so Bannock ushered his two companions down the steps and then followed on behind. It mattered not that the lookout had been withdrawn, because he was confident that they would not hear from the Comanches again that night. Even they had to sleep sometime!

115

*

Daylight revealed a sad state of affairs in the isolated settlement of San Marcos. The various fires had burnt themselves out, and now only wisps of dark smoke drifted up from the uninhabitable buildings. The fact that they had survived to see another day wasn't sufficient to check the despondency that was spreading over the peons and their families. And that negative emotion showed itself in a suggestion made to Luis that was swiftly relayed to his guest.

'Some of the men are talking of maybe surrendering to avoid any more destruction to their property.'

Bannock spat expressively into the dust. Like everyone else, he hadn't slept much that night, but such suggestions could not be allowed to stand.

'Then they must have shit for brains,' he snarled. 'This isn't a war between gentlemen. There ain't no surrendering to those devils.'

'But could we not make a truce?'

'You mean parley with them?'

Luis nodded eagerly. His tired features were coated with dust and ash.

'And what of your children?' Bannock demanded. 'Do you all really care so little for them?'

The peon was baffled. 'You talk in riddles, *señor.*'

The American guffawed loudly, but little warmth reached his eyes. 'I'll allow that they *might* just be thinking that taking this place ain't worth the return anymore. But, if you try to make terms with them, they'll demand tribute, for sure.'

'They already have our cattle!'

'It ain't livestock they're short of. It's children. Smallpox has killed more Comanches than any number of Texas Rangers. Their little ones don't have any immunity to it, but other folks's children do. Savvy?'

Luis's eyes registered genuine horror, as he glanced over to where his daughter was sleeping. 'I could never let them take her,' he announced, with every sign of renewed resolve.

'Others have felt that way,' Bannock muttered grimly, as he suddenly recalled the little girl and her red bonnet. 'And the only way to avoid it is to keep fighting, because sooner or later I reckon those horse Indians are gonna tire of all this.'

He had spoken with every display of conviction, but deep down the American wasn't so sure. There was something different about this band. It was as though their leader had got it into his head to finish the job, regardless of cost. But surely the notoriously independent Comanches wouldn't just blindly follow on.

Set-tainte was indeed having problems of his own. His warriors weren't accustomed to enduring heavy casualties. It didn't sit well with many of them. And it appeared that Alaki had been chosen for the unenviable job of mounting a challenge.

'We have many dead, with nothing more to show for it than a herd of scrawny cattle,' he declared, his hawklike features set and determined. He did not relish his task. Set-tainte was a fearsome war chief of great repute, but Alaki knew that he had the backing of many in the

117

band. 'I say we should leave these pathetic creatures to their worthless existence. There will be another day, when they do not have that *Tejano* with them.'

Set-tainte's eyes narrowed dangerously. 'And what about our dead? Do we not avenge them?'

'How?' spat back the other. 'They are behind walls, armed with guns. That damned ranger, or whatever he is, never misses. *You* might have become obsessed with him, but we have had enough!'

The chief's eyes seemed to glisten in the harsh sunlight. 'Who is *we*?'

Suddenly horribly aware of the rising tension, Alaki licked his lips nervously. He glanced around at his fellow warriors for support. Some were clustered around him, keen to see the outcome of the confrontation. Others had distanced themselves from it by tending to their ponies, or lounging by the campfires. The contender gestured at those nearest to him. 'I speak for them.'

Set-tainte's thin lips twisted slightly. 'Yet I hear only your words.'

Unexpectedly he abruptly crooked his left forefinger, summoning the other man closer. 'And so my reply should be for your ears only.'

Almost hypnotized by the penetrating gaze, Alaki involuntarily moved closer, leaning forward as he did so. Like a striking snake, Set-tainte's left hand curled around the back of his unsuspecting opponent's head, seized hold of a clump of jet black hair and pulled hard. At the same time, the chief's right knee snapped up, catching his victim's face full on with tremendous force. Every warrior in camp heard the bone break in Alaki's nose. Excruciating pain exploded around his eyes, and for a few crucial seconds he was completely helpless.

Maintaining a vice-like grip on his hair, Set-tainte brutally heaved him up and around, so that the unfortunate warrior ended up facing his distressingly unsupportive comrades. With blood and mucus streaming from his wrecked nose, Alaki never saw the knife that appeared at his throat, but he sure as hell felt it. As the razor-sharp blade dug in, drawing yet more blood, the damage to his face suddenly paled into insignificance.

'Who else thinks as he does?' Set-tainte demanded.

His warriors thrived on hunting and warfare. They were hardened to killing, but they were also used to being led . . . by the man before them. They had never questioned his leadership before, and they were beginning to doubt the wisdom of attempting it now. Nevertheless, they did have genuine grievances.

'Too many of our brothers won't see their families again,' one of them protested.

Set-tainte nodded understandingly, but his grip never slackened. 'It is true. Many have lost their lives that shouldn't have, but we could not have foreseen that. What we can do is avenge them.' His hooded eyes roamed over them. 'Who amongst you could just ride away, knowing that that white man, the killer of our people, is still drawing breath?'

The assembled warriors glanced at each other uncomfortably. There were undoubtedly many who wished to do just that, but their leader had laid down a direct challenge, and any man who shied away from it risked belittling himself before his peers.

Set-tainte fully understood the effect of his words, and now it was time to reveal his intentions. 'If I told you that I had a plan to take that accursed place, would you still follow me?'

The assembled warriors returned their full attention to him. Or rather what they could see of him behind the bloodied and helpless figure of their comrade. Gradually, and in some cases very reluctantly, they all nodded their assent.

'So how do we go about it?' one of them demanded.

A hint of a smile creased Set-tainte's harsh features. 'Simple. We will torment the Mexicans with more fire, and then give them their cattle back.' And with that, he removed the bloodstained blade from Alaki's throat, allowing him to slump to earth, hurting but mercifully still alive.

CHAPTER TEN

The defendants of San Marcos had not expected to hear gunfire from beyond their walls. The Comanches possessed few firearms, and certainly nothing that could penetrate adobe. And yet, later on that morning, someone was firing a repeater. Knowing that another attack was almost certain, the American had been back on the undamaged section of wall since his impassioned conversation with Luis. What he now saw caused his heart to skip a beat.

A lone rider, apparently white, was spurring his horse towards the beleaguered settlement. Bannock's first thought was that it was a cunning ruse, and that a Comanche had got dressed up in stolen clothes. But no, it was indeed a white man. And he sure had stirred up a hornet's nest.

'Rider coming in, and he ain't an Indian,' he bellowed down to a startled Luis. 'Get one of those gates shifted.' He noticed the old-timer with the sawn-off staring up at him expectantly and grinned, before gesturing for him to ascend the stairs. At least someone was up for a fight!

Barely had the gate been heaved aside, than the lone fugitive burst into the compound. Bannock levelled his rifle at the pursuers, but they rapidly veered off. Knowing his deadly skill with a long gun, they weaved skilfully from side to side to disrupt his aim. He shrugged philosophically, and held fire, unwilling to waste precious powder. There'd be another time.

The new arrival reined in and then swung his panting animal around in a full circle, so as to allow an inspection of his unfamiliar surroundings. Incongruously for such harsh terrain, he sported a dark frockcoat, which had once been expensive, but was now worn and travel stained. Likewise, his riding boots hinted at someone who had been a man of means, but was now down on his luck. Unless, of course, the whole attire had merely been stolen.

As he took in the sea of anxious faces, men, women and children too, his dust-coated features contorted into a strange leer. The action was emphasized by a livid scar on his left cheek, which had effectively ended his chances of ever being considered handsome. To the more perceptive there, it was noticeable that the young women claimed most of his attention. But such scrutiny was short-lived, because then something very strange occurred.

Almost simultaneously, Bannock descended the stairs as the stranger dismounted, so that they suddenly came face to face with roughly ten yards separating them. As their eyes met, both men uttered the same word. 'You!'

Each of them went for their nearest firearm, before seeming to recollect that they were not alone by any means. All around them, the villagers looked on in stunned amazement. As though frozen in time, their stares were locked together with malevolent intensity, but neither of them actually levelled a weapon. Somehow, the knowledge of the external threat still managed to penetrate their mutual loathing.

It was Bannock who finally broke the deadlock. 'I thought you was dead, you back-shooting cockchafer!'

'So did I . . . until I realized I was just in Texas,' retorted the other harshly, his expression completely devoid of humour. 'And besides, that charge was never proven.'

Another period of strained silence followed, as though each man was willing the other to make the first move.

'You look like you're fixing to pop a cap on me,' the newcomer finally continued.

'I'll allow I'm considering it,' Bannock retorted.

'Whatever happened to that big bastard, Butler?'

'He didn't make it.'

'Shame. I'd hoped it would be me that paroled him to Jesus.'

'You're all heart, Braxton.'

'Yeah, I know. It's a weakness of mine.'

Their tense standoff showed no sign of ending, but suddenly there was a cry from the wall, as outside forces again took a hand. '*Señor, señor*. Los Comanches, they move!'

The scarred visitor shrugged. 'Looks like this'll have to wait.'

'Yeah,' Bannock snapped, as he abruptly swivelled on his heels and made for the wall, at the same time yelling, 'Get that damn gate back in place!'

From his familiar vantage point he could see that the Comanches were indeed on the move, but their intentions were far from obvious. This time they had split into two groups. One party moved round towards the far wall, but kept beyond easy rifle range. The others made off at speed into the surrounding hills.

'Those devils are cooking up something,' he muttered almost to himself.

Then he suddenly found Luis at his shoulder, his honest features perplexed.

'Who is that *hombre, señor*?'

'Oh, he's that all right,' Bannock replied with feeling. 'I don't know what he's calling himself at the moment, but his real name is Braxton. Silas Braxton.'

'I don't think he likes you.'

'You could tell, huh?'

The mild attempt at humour was lost on the Mexican. 'But what would bring him to San Marcos?'

'I reckon he's probably on the dodge.'

There was a limit to the other man's language skills. 'Dodge. What is this dodge?'

'Don't you folks know it's rude to whisper?' Braxton called up. 'Seems like I'm gonna be staying in this shit hole for a while, what with those Comanches out there, an' all. So where can I stable my horse? He needs food and a good rub down. A bit like me,' he added suggestively, his eyes drifting off to settle on a young *señorita*.

Before anyone could answer him, events beyond the

124

settlement once more intruded. The Indians beyond the far wall had dismounted to create a small blaze, and were igniting a number of fire arrows. It was now all too obvious what their intentions were, and unfortunately there was no feasible way to stop them. The mission walls had not really been built with vigorous defence in mind. No firing steps had been provided, or even any kind of walkway on the wall behind the church. Their assailants would be able to torch the structures on that side with impunity.

'Looks like it's all starting again,' Bannock grimly announced to Luis. 'Tell everyone to clear out of those buildings.' Then he turned and peered off to where the other band had disappeared. Instinctively he knew that something else was brewing.

Recognizing that any interest in him had abruptly ceased, Braxton grunted and remarked, 'Guess I'll just make my own arrangements then. It sure is a real pleasure visiting with you folks.' And with that he spat a stream of yellow phlegm into the dust, before taking the reins of his horse and leading it towards the former church. Located more centrally in the compound, it seemed to offer rather more protection . . . at least for the moment.

Gleefully unleashing a range of demonic howls, the Comanches rapidly closed in until they were just outside the far wall. With complete impunity, they loosed a wave of fire arrows at the timber roof supports. These had baked under the sun for years, and the result was all too predictable: soon light grey smoke began to curl up into the sky.

For the villagers it was all immensely traumatic. They were soon to be without a roof over their heads – but Bannock had even more pressing concerns. From the side facing the main entrance came the thrumming of many hoofs: San Marcos's herd of cattle was returning . . . at an even faster pace than when they had been stolen! Comanche warriors accompanied them at their rear and along their flanks, tightly controlling the direction, and screaming wildly to keep them moving. It was obvious what their intentions were.

Knowing that the 'lean-to' gates couldn't withstand such a collision, the American's response was unsurprising: 'Oh, shit!'

Turning to the terrified lookout, he patted him on the shoulder and pointed to the stairs. 'Seems like we're all done up here, my friend.'

Whether the villager had understood any of that, mattered not. He had seen the same sight that Bannock had. He, too, recognized what was coming, and his response was to sketch the universally recognized sign of the cross. Then together they trotted down the stairs, and across the compound.

Luis held his daughter in one hand and a machete in the other, as he watched the American's rapid approach. He had been around him long enough to know that, from his expression, they were all in deep trouble.

'The sons of bitches are fixing on stampeding your cattle through the gates. Then they'll surely follow them in. And this time we've got neither surprise, nor enough of anything else to stop them. Our only chance is to fort up in that church, but if they fire the roof . . .' He shrugged, and left the sentence unfinished. There really wasn't anything else to say.

As though emphasizing their likely fate, the timber cross-beams known as *lattillas*, which were themselves covered in extremely flammable brushwood, began to crackle as the flames really took hold. Very soon there wouldn't be a habitable building left in the settlement.

The man known as Silas Braxton, amongst other things, rubbed his horse down and pondered his parlous situation. It really appeared as though he had leapt out of the frying pan straight into the fire. Quite literally, as it was shaping up. And he certainly hadn't expected to run into an old adversary in such a Godforsaken spot. At the thought of Bannock, his left hand reflexively touched the scar on his cheek. He wondered if any of the locals had discovered that individual's given name yet. 'Highly unlikely,' he muttered to himself. Perhaps he would have to enlighten them. The thought brought a chill smile to his damaged features.

Then his attention was taken by the sudden influx of residents, clutching whatever belongings they had managed to salvage, and he instinctively knew what was occurring: this was the designated 'last stand', and by great ill fortune he had stumbled into it with impeccable timing. He wasn't a man to ponder on 'if onlys', but there was no denying that he should probably have taken his chances in the open. As it was, he certainly had more to worry about than a long-standing feud with his fellow countryman.

At that moment, Bannock himself entered the church and called over to him. 'We ain't overly endowed with firearms, so right now you'd help yourself if you helped us.' He waited a moment for Braxton to close in, and then added more quietly, 'You and me have got matters that need settling, but this ain't the time. Agreed?'

The newcomer viewed him through narrowed eyes for a moment, before nodding slowly. 'I reckon.' He continued to regard the other man speculatively. 'So how's this gonna pan out?'

Bannock kept his voice low. 'In truth, I believe we're well and truly screwed. But this is the hand that we've been dealt, so we'll just have to go with it. If nothing else, I owe it to that little girl with the red dress.'

Braxton's eyebrows rose in surprise. The child was way too young for it to be sexual. 'Kin?'

'Nah. Just down to something that happened a few days ago. Seems like a lifetime away now.' Bannock shook his head, as though trying to clear a persistent and unwelcome memory. There was certainly no desire on his part to share confidences with such a man. 'I could use your Colts at the entrance,' he continued briskly. 'There's no point in barricading the door, 'cause if those devils fire the roof we're all finished. Our only chance is to keep them at a distance.' Even as he spoke, he knew that their chances of achieving that were slim and, as the rather weak joke went, 'Slim had just left town!'

*

Galloping by the side of the terrified cattle, Set-tainte was suffused with elation. Fiercely, he lashed out with the short whip that he habitually carried. There was surely nothing to exceed the joy of warfare. Not even the pleasuring of his wives. And with his warriors around him, and the enemy's walls fast approaching, there was nowhere else he would rather be.

Too late, the leading animals saw the solid objects ahead and frantically tried to turn away, but they were hemmed in on three sides. With a tremendous crash, that literally snapped the necks of the two front-runners, the herd ploughed into the gates, smashing them aside. Those behind trampled over the hapless creatures brought down in front, and raced on into the compound, followed by the jubilant Comanches. Above them still sat the severed head of their comrade. Having dried out somewhat under the strong sun, it now bore a macabre fixed grin, but on this occasion they didn't even glance at it. The carnage of the previous assault was still too raw in their minds, and their attention was elsewhere, searching intently for any resistance. And yet this time there were no lethal, hidden powder charges, or concealed ropes waiting to trip them. Just wrecked or burning buildings.

Nevertheless, the chief wasn't taking any more chances with the lives of his warriors. Sharply reining in, he signalled for them to do the same. Ahead of him there were only winded and suddenly aimless cattle, and what he recognized as a sometime place of worship for the Mexican missionaries. Quickly coming to a decision, he barked out a series of commands.

Half a dozen warriors urged their mounts forwards. With great skill, they hung down over the sides of their animals, so that only their hands and feet were visible. Using the Mexicans' livestock as cover, they advanced on the large building. Immediately, shots rang out, and at least two cows crumpled to the ground. The Indians performed a rapid U turn and raced away. Their brief foray had told them all they needed to know.

Set-tainte nodded his head in satisfaction. The entrance to the building was strongly defended, but with there being no windows or even an open bell tower, it was the only part that was. The warriors who had fired the buildings were now streaming expectantly into the compound. The chief's broad smile displayed his genuine good humour. He had more work for them. And the sure knowledge that they were going to prevail brought savage joy to his heart.

Waving the new arrivals off to the right, and so out of sight of any gunmen, he then pointed at the church roof and bared his teeth. Not a man amongst them failed to take his meaning. Quickly they gathered together the makings for a small fire, and then lit it from one of the blazing roof timbers. Revenge was indeed going to be sweet. In particular, the sickly sweet smell of burning flesh!

After the swiftly curtailed sortie by the mounted Indians, Bannock knew exactly what was coming next. He and those with firearms were crouched behind a makeshift barricade, inside the church's entrance. Their severely restricted field of fire was a lethal weakness, for which there was only really one answer. Looking back into the body of the church, he saw the villagers observing him nervously. The men clasped their rudimentary weapons, whilst the women clutched their children. Then he spotted Pepita's red dress, and his stomach churned uncomfortably.

'God damn it! Why has it come to this?' he silently demanded of himself.

Knowing that there could be no good answer to that, the American glanced over at the Paterson Colt revolvers in Braxton's hands. They were identical to his, and he recalled from experience that that man was well skilled in their use.

'Hey, Braxton,' he called. 'How's about you an' me taking on those heathen sons of bitches? Either that, or we all burn to death in here.'

Braxton regarded him impassively. 'Since you put it like that, how can I refuse?' Gesturing at his surroundings, he added, 'I've never had any call for religion anyhu. Just don't get behind me with those belt guns. Savvy?'

'Backshooting's not my style,' retorted the other man. 'You of all men should know that.'

Braxton's facial scar twitched slightly. 'Now there you go again. On the prod.' Even as he spoke, he was checking the loads in his revolvers.

Nearby, Tomas was clutching the Hawken. It had been temporarily returned to him, because he at least knew how to use it. The old-timer with the sawn-off was also behind the barricade, along with another peon who had been entrusted with Bannock's captured musket.

As the two *gringos* stood up, Bannock called back to Luis. 'Tell these three to give us covering fire. Oh, and if I don't make it back, Tomas gets to keep the rifle.' Then he added under his breath, 'Not that those devils will let him have it for long.'

After winking encouragingly at Pepita, he reluctantly turned to his dubious ally. 'Anyone with a fire arrow, blast them!'

'I didn't come down with yesterday's rain,' snarled Braxton. 'Save your advice for these poxy greasers. They might actually give a damn!' With that, he cocked both Colts and gestured outside. 'Let's get this done!'

CHAPTER ELEVEN

The two desperate men burst out of the church and turned to their left. Even though possessing four of the most potent weapons available, they still had only twenty shots available in total. And that presupposed that there would be no misfires. All in all, they had taken a hell of a lot upon themselves!

Old hands at fighting, they remained a few yards apart, so as to present less of a target. Even though terribly outnumbered, there was something predatory about their rapid advance. With no cover of any kind, they were dreadfully exposed, but knew that they had to concentrate on the fire starters. At the very least, they might be able to delay the inevitable. It was what was known in the God-damned British Army as a 'forlorn hope'.

The Comanches were taken completely by surprise. They couldn't possibly have expected such a suicidal assault on foot, because it was something *they* wouldn't even consider under any circumstances.

Bannock was the first to shoot. His ball struck a

warrior standing near the small fire that the Indians had created. By great good fortune it killed the man stone dead, *and* sent him tumbling on to the flames, completely smothering them. Then his companion opened up with both Colts simultaneously, striking a pony in the belly and a warrior in the shoulder. Damn good shooting for a man on the move.

'Kill anyone with a bow,' Bannock bellowed, momentarily forgetting that he was partnering an experienced man killer.

'They've all got bows, an' I don't need telling,' Braxton yelled back.

And yet, the first part of that retort was not strictly true, because at that moment one particular warrior's treasured status symbol, an old Brown Bess cavalry carbine, was being aimed directly at him. With its outdated flintlock mechanism, it harked back to a bygone era, but it could still be dangerous, as it was about to demonstrate. There was a flash as, miraculously, the powder ignited in the pan, and a large calibre ball flew at the indignant American. With a tremendous clang, it struck the barrel of his right-hand Colt, just as he was in the act of cocking it. The revolver was torn from his grasp with such force that he nearly fell over. As it was, Braxton was badly shaken and had obviously lost the use of his hand.

Thrusting one gun in his belt, Bannock instinctively closed in, and reached out to steady the other man, whilst at the same time searching out another target. Ignoring the 'musketeer', who had expended his single shot, he fired at another archer. The ball gorily removed the top of the warrior's head, and pitched him backwards to the hard ground with a great thump.

'Unhand me, damn it,' Braxton rasped. 'I ain't some poxy invalid.' So saying, he pulled clear of Bannock's grip, and took rapid aim with his remaining Colt. Although in great pain, his ball nevertheless winged one of their assailants.

Now side by side, in a cloud of acrid smoke, the two men stood their ground and kept firing. But they had lost a little of their momentum, and there were just too many Indians opposing them. Then, from the back of the church, a flaming arrow arced across the sky and slammed squarely into one of that building's roof supports. The archer had obviously lit it from the existing fires, and that action effectively doomed the Americans' desperate offensive.

Braxton's hammer struck an empty nipple, announcing that he had used his five. His other revolver lay on the ground, mangled beyond repair. With the Comanches recovering their natural aggression, it was time to return to the dubious safety of the church.

'You first. I'll cover you,' Bannock instructed.

'You just love to give orders, don't you?' Braxton rejoined, but nonetheless he turned towards the entrance.

Bannock, now alone and feeling increasingly isolated, crouched down to make a smaller target. As he did so, he felt a searing pain as something cut across his right cheek. Had he remained standing, it would undoubtedly have struck his torso full on. With blood trickling over his jaw line, and mounted Indians getting ever closer, he decided that he had given Braxton long enough. Then his right-hand Colt dry-fired, and a disciplined retreat was suddenly out of the question. Turning on his heels, he ran for cover, weaving from side to side to disrupt his opponents' aim.

Those Comanches nearest to him yelled loudly and dug their heels in. Grimly expecting the inevitable barbed arrowhead to slam into his back, Bannock could feel prickles of anxiety flow down it. Then, unbelievably, he saw two figures move towards him. One was the grizzled old peon with his twelve-gauge, whilst the other proved to be Tomas. Bannock glimpsed the Hawken in his hands as one might recognize an old friend.

As the fleeing *gringo* came level with them, first one shotgun barrel and then the second discharged with a rolling crash. As a useful amount of smoke erupted between them and the Comanches, the long rifle also belched forth its own particular brand of death. As screams of pain came from their mutual enemy, Bannock found himself under cover, and joined by his two rescuers. He nodded and smiled his grateful thanks. Safe again – but for how long?

Set-tainte watched in disbelief as the white man disappeared within the adobe walls. It really appeared as though he was protected by some higher power. Yet not even that would save him from the blazing inferno that was about to follow. Waving his bleeding and frustrated warriors back from the entrance, he bellowed at those nearest the rear of the building to send more fire arrows into the timber beams. Once the roof fell in, there would be nowhere else left for the surviving villagers to hide. Those that weren't burnt to death would find him and his men waiting for them. And then he would surely get to try out his new, seven-barrelled gun. The prospect of unleashing that monstrous weapon on defenceless Mexicans brought a flush of pleasure to his bronzed features.

Bannock's return had been greeted by a sea of anxious, questioning faces, but he hadn't known what to say to them. 'We're all going to burn to death,' translated into Spanish, didn't seem adequate somehow, and so instead he had said nothing.

Now, as he tried to staunch the blood flowing from his cheek, he looked up and saw smoke appearing above him. The roof level was a lot higher than in the other buildings, but that wouldn't save them once the fire really took hold. Sensing movement beside him, he turned to find Silas Braxton staring at him, all the while massaging his obviously painful right hand.

'What you did out there hasn't changed anything between us, you know,' that man rasped.

'I wouldn't have it any other way,' Bannock retorted, although in truth he didn't really care. All he could think about was the horrible fate that awaited them all, but more especially Pepita in her lovely red dress.

'God damn it to hell!' he suddenly exclaimed to no one in particular. 'There must be something we can do.' Glancing around, he spotted Luis. 'Have you any water in here?'

That man shrugged. 'A little, *señor.*'

'Try to wet the ceiling. It might delay the fire.'

Bannock wouldn't have blamed the Mexican if he'd replied, 'Delay the fire for what?' But he didn't. What he did do was instruct his people to get the earthenware pots of water, and start splashing it above them. It was a pitiful enough defence, but at least it would keep them occupied.

'Not all of it, mind,' the American added. He well knew that there would be another use for it once the flames really took hold.

'What say we make a break for it? Just you and me,' Braxton enquired softly. 'Leave these damn peasants to fry in their own grease. If we break out together, and use that scattergun, we might just make it. Them Comanches don't much like hot lead. Steal a couple of ponies, and then once away from this shit hole, we can finally settle our differences.' His uninjured hand brushed the scar on his cheek. 'Way I see it, even after all this, I still owe you some grief.'

Bannock stared at him scornfully. 'I reckon not. Unlike you, when I side with someone, I stick with them!'

A sneer spread across the other man's harsh features. 'So that's how it is. Well, it don't take much understanding. I seen how you've been eyeing that little bitch over there.'

Bannock's habitual self-control abruptly snapped. Without warning, he lashed out with a vicious backhand slap across Braxton's face, and then followed it up with a tremendous blow to his jaw. That man reeled backwards, falling on to a long table that then collapsed under his weight.

'Stay down, you cockchafer,' Bannock snarled. ' 'Cause if you get up, so help me God, I'll kill you stone dead!' As it turned out, he was wasting his breath. Braxton was out cold, and likely to stay that way for some time. Up above, the flames were spreading, making a mockery of the villagers' frantic efforts. 'Looks like you'll just have to take your chances,' he muttered and turned to walk away. But then some little niggle in the recesses of his mind brought him up short. Regardless of who it was, he just couldn't let someone burn to death. Somehow that would seem worse still than any amount of back-shooting.

Sighing, Bannock decided to at least afford Braxton a fighting chance, even though knowing that he couldn't have expected the same courtesy from him. Seizing the solid tabletop, he placed it over the prone figure, and then again turned away. The man's chances were now probably little worse than all the others trapped in the building.

The heaviest beams, the vigas, were ablaze, as were the other supports. What Bannock had feared most was now happening: there was nowhere left to run to, and their holdout position was about to come down on their heads.

'Forget that,' he yelled at Luis. 'Nothing will stop it. Tell everyone to dip some clothing in water and hold it over their faces. Then get them to lie on the floor around the base of the walls. It's all we can do.'

Luis shook his head in despair, but translated the instructions anyway. Then, bringing Pepita with him, he joined the solitary American over by the nearest wall. All around them the villagers did the same. The heat was becoming unbearable. Hot ashes were dropping down to the dirt floor, and it was only a matter of time before the whole roof followed. Considering the dire situation, there was very little panic. It was as though the bloody events of the last day or so had somehow anaesthetized them against further trauma.

As the three of them huddled down together, the Mexican peered at him questioningly. He had Pepita's trembling body wrapped tightly in his arms. She held a damp cloth over her face. The noise and heat made conversation difficult, but there was something he just had to ask. 'Tell me honestly, *señor*. Would all this destruction have happened if you hadn't come among us?'

Bannock's eyes widened slightly. That was a hell of a question to have to answer, but he owed it to the man to try. 'No,' he emphatically replied. 'No, it wouldn't. Because your resistance would have been far less. But all that means is that they would have killed any men that they chose, and then carried off the women and children too for their own ends. At least this way you've had a fighting chance . . . and it *could* have worked out. Comanches ain't normally this persistent.'

At that moment, before Luis had any chance to respond, the structure above began to give way. With a great crash, a large section of burning timber fell into the centre of the one-room building. Daylight flooded in from above, and along with it came much of the remaining roof. Flaming brushwood showered down, landing on and igniting the former church's rudimentary furniture. The intense heat suddenly became unendurable. For the desperate villagers, their unprotected flesh blistering agonizingly, whatever awaited them outside couldn't possibly be worse. And so, en masse, they despairingly staggered to their feet and made for the entrance.

Outside, the gleeful Comanches sat their ponies in a semi-circle and waited. Their barbed arrows were ready, and this time Set-tainte felt confident that there would be no resistance worthy of the name. The slaughter would be glorious, and whoever they chose to spare would be enslaved. Just as had always been the case!

CHAPTER TWELVE

'*Disparar!*'

The ragged volley that crashed out was so totally unexpected that for a long, crucial moment the only Comanches to react were the dead and dying. Even when they did turn to view their unknown assailants, it was not immediately apparent just who they were up against. A great cloud of powder smoke was only gradually clearing from the area near the main entrance. Behind it, they were able to glimpse snatches of blue and white material.

This brief period of uncharacteristic inactivity gave *Capitan* Ugalde's fifty regulars the crucial time they needed to recharge their muzzle-loaders. It was a very rare occurrence for Mexican infantry to catch horse Indians in an enclosed space, and he fully intended to make the most of it. His tired, sweating men had made a forced march to reach San Marcos, but all that was forgotten as they presented their weapons to unleash another volley.

With a further deafening crash, fifty muskets dis-

142

charged into the relatively small area before the wrecked church. Set-tainte watched with horror as, mere feet away, a massive .69-calibre lead ball totally destroyed Alaki's already battered features. Miraculously the war chief remained untouched, but all around him far too many of his warriors had been blasted from their ponies. He still couldn't quite grasp just what was happening, and had no idea how to tackle the apparently overwhelming force arrayed against his people. Then he saw a line of wicked-looking bayonets advance through the 'fog of war', and he abruptly realized that all was lost.

Standing a little off to the side, Ugalde had noticed that a number of survivors were beginning to emerge from the church. He could no longer risk another volley, and so had given the order to advance. As his men tramped slowly, purposefully forwards, the officer could sense that the Comanches were broken. Taken by surprise, the remaining warriors couldn't stand against even moderately disciplined soldiers.

The muffled roar of gunfire came as just one more shock to those in the ruined church, but it could make no difference to their decision to flee. To remain was to die, pure and simple.

Bannock, wearing thicker clothing than the others, was using his back to shield Luis and Pepita, as they made their way around the wall to the exit. The sickly smell of burning flesh reached his nostrils, as some of those at the rear succumbed to the flames, but there could be no help for them. He had no idea who could be firing, but was very conscious of the fact that he hadn't had a chance to reload any of his weapons. All he could do was brandish them threateningly, and hope that the Comanches would seek easier victims.

As the three of them stumbled out into the open, the American peered around guardedly. He fully expected to be attacked immediately, but amazingly it was the Comanches who were on the defensive... those few that remained. Then he looked to his left and saw the extended bayonets of their saviours approaching. 'Hot damn,' he murmured wondrously. This was one turn of events that he could never have envisaged. And yet it wasn't *quite* over.

As he saw the hated white man emerge into the sunlight, Set-tainte let out a guttural snarl. If he achieved nothing else that day, he would at least kill one particular individual. Even after thumbing back the hammer on his prized volleygun, it still required both hands to hold and aim the massive weapon, and so he controlled his animal by leg pressure alone. That presented no problem, because like all his kind, he was an expert rider. Fully intending to see the expression on his victim's face as he was blown to pieces, the obsessed war chief moved into point-blank range.

As Luis and Pepita staggered away from his protective mantel, Bannock sensed the sudden movement directly before him. Looking up, he found himself staring into the gaping muzzles of Chet's treasured Nock, and his heart sank.

Set-tainte bared his teeth in a feral grin, and

squeezed the trigger. The powder in the pan flashed satisfactorily, and then there was an ear-splitting roar as the fearsome, but incorrectly loaded weapon quite literally blew up in his face. Shards of metal turned his features into a bloody pulp, but others also struck both his torso and the animal beneath him. Rearing up in pain, it unceremoniously deposited its dead rider on to the hard ground like so much rubbish, before racing off across the compound.

Bannock gazed down at the mutilated Comanche who had tried so hard to kill him, and observed 'Huh! Looks like Chet Butler had the final say after all!'

No one else heard him, because the remaining villagers were all staring in amazement as the *soldados* advanced across the front of the church, their bayonets driving the last Indians before them. The warriors made no attempt to resist with their bows. Their defeat had turned into a rout, and all they could think of was to escape over the nearest low wall. Without a backward glance, they raced off to the north-east, and the eventual safety of Comancheria. Unusually for a war party, they were lacking scalps, livestock, captives . . . and their own leader!

Capitan Ugalde carefully scrutinized the surrounding settlement, occasionally shaking his head in disbelief. He had never seen the like before. Admittedly, burnt-out villages were not unusual in northern Mexico, after the one-sided raids by horse Indians, but this was very different. San Marcos resembled a battlefield. Resistance had been extreme, and evidence of that was the severed head of a Comanche warrior, still displayed over the main entrance. Not to mention the array of blood-drenched cadavers that had been present before his men had even opened fire.

The *capitan* was not a harsh man by any means. In fact, he was known for both his humanity and sense of justice. It was the former that had compelled him into confronting *Coronel* Vallejo, and persuading that self-centred officer into allowing a detachment of fifty men to return to San Marcos.

Paradoxically, it was exactly because of the latter quality that he had to override his natural sympathy for the distraught villagers, and put military matters first.

Ugalde had many questions that required answers. *Sargento* Montoya's murder remained unsolved, and he believed that the solution might well be found in the settlement. He was also greatly puzzled by the presence of a lone *Americano*. This man had not been there the last time they had been in the settlement. Or at least he hadn't been *seen* then. Could it be that it was he who had instigated such an unusually stubborn defence . . . amongst other things?

'*Teniente!*' he called out. Moments later, Felipe stood before him. The young man appeared to be somewhat queasy at the sight of so much blood and gore, but he would learn to cope. He would have to. He was a pro-fessional soldier!

Ugalde issued a series of orders. 'Post lookouts on the walls where possible. Round up any Indian ponies within the compound and use them to drag the bodies outside.'

'To bury them, *mi capitan*?'

Ugalde stared at him incredulously, before shaking his head. 'Soldados of Mexico do not dig holes for savages. Pile them high and burn them all.'

The colour drained from Felipe's youthful features, and he swallowed uncomfortably. '*Sí, mi capitan.*' About to turn away, a thought suddenly came to him. 'The burning buildings. What should we do about them?'

'Nothing. They are too far gone. Just let the fires burn out. Then these people will have to choose whether to leave or rebuild. Either way, we won't be here then. We have given them their lives, and that is all we can do.'

Thoroughly chastened, the *teniente* saluted and turned away. This was one campaign he would not forget in a hurry.

Silas Braxton felt as though his entire body was on fire. The agony engulfing him was intense, but at least it meant that he was still alive. But how could that be, when it seemed as though the whole roof had collapsed on him? Tentatively, he shifted his shoulders, and discovered that some form of table or bench lay across them. This must have protected him from the worst of the flames. With other things to contend with, he gave no thought as to how it might have got there.

Groaning with the effort, Braxton shifted his arms under his chest to gain some leverage. Burning brushwood tumbled from his temporary shield, and fell on either side of him. Christ, but he'd been lucky! With an abrupt heave, he scrambled on to all fours, and then tilted sideways. Whatever was on his back fell to the ground, and it felt as though the weight of the world had been lifted from him. Yet the intense heat remained. He had painful blisters on his face and hands. It was past time to move, and yet his innate caution remained. In spite of his dire circumstances, he dimly recalled registering an outbreak of heavy gunfire, followed by some kind of explosion. Even though that had all now passed, he sensed that some important change had take place beyond his four walls.

After cautiously getting to his feet, Braxton moved rapidly over to the exit, but did not go outside. The stench in his nostrils told him that not everybody had survived the blaze, but all those still living appeared to have fled, so he had the wrecked premises to himself. Since the flames were subsiding, he decided to stay put and wait on events. There seemed to be a deal of activity in the compound, so it made sense to play dead and rely on his 'listeners' for a time. If he had done that during his recent debacle in Santa Fe, he wouldn't have been on the run in the first place, and hence almost burnt to death in Sonora!

As the officer's gaze again returned to him, Bannock could feel the familiar itch down his back that was usually an infallible warning of trouble. All around him, the villagers either sat or squatted, devoid of all energy. They appeared barely able to believe that it was all over, and seemed to have neither the desire nor ability to celebrate the fact. Perhaps they were just overwhelmed by the enormity of the reconstruction task that lay ahead of them. One thing was for sure; none of *them* were the subject of the *capitan*'s intense scrutiny!

'So we survived, *señor*. Most of us, anyway.' Luis remarked bitterly, as he peered up at the *Americano*. The peon's expression was hard to read. A strange mixture of anxiety, disbelief and exhaustion. Curled up in his lap, little Pepita slept soundly. That was surely the best thing for her. She had experienced things that would undoubtedly stay with her for the rest of her life. 'But will those devils return, once you and the *soldados* have left? Will there be any point in rebuilding?'

Bannock could at least answer that with certainty. 'You won't see them or any other Comanches again. I know a little of how they think. They respect strength in an enemy. Word of their defeat here will spread. San Marcos will become known as a place of bad medicine for them, to be avoided at all costs. So at least something good has come out of all this bloodshed.'

Luis's eyes widened with surprise and genuine pleasure. 'Really? So all this wasn't for nothing?'

A peculiar look came over Bannock. 'What I've found in the past is that when the shooting stops, and the dead are buried, none of it means anything. So you build this place up again, and damn well prove me wrong! You hear?'

For the first time in days, a bright smile lit up the Mexican's sallow features. 'You're a strange one, *patron*. But yes, we will rebuild. San Marcos will be a home for us all to be proud of again. *You'll* see.'

With his peripheral vision, Bannock could make out a figure in blue, with a smattering of gold and scarlet, approaching their position. 'I've a feeling I might not be around for that,' he muttered darkly.

Capitan Ugalde arrived in front of them, flanked by two burly *privados*. For all his lack of arrogance, he never doubted that he was the master there. He required answers, and he would have them, because of all those remaining in San Marcos who might have murdered Montoya, this lean, hard-faced Anglo appeared the most likely.

'Your name, *señor*?' he asked in strongly accented, but nevertheless perfect English.

The other man regarded him silently for a moment. Dried blood coated his right cheek, emphasizing his somewhat menacing demeanour. 'Bannock,' he eventually replied, his hard eyes no longer downcast or averted.

Ugalde regarded him speculatively. 'And what brings you to San Marcos, Señor Bannock?'

It was Luis who, somewhat too eagerly, answered that. He unquestionably meant well, but as it turned out Bannock was to wish that he'd just kept quiet. 'This man kept us alive until you returned, *patron*. He is a great *pistolero*. It was he who cut the head off the Comanche devil. We owe him a great debt.'

The *capitan* nodded indulgently. 'Very impressive, to be sure,' he murmured, before allowing his tone to harden perceptibly. 'But that is not what I asked. Nor did I ask you!'

Bannock sighed wearily. Some instinct told him not to mention the wagon train, so he kept it simple. 'I'd had a run-in some time before with the same war party,

150

and came here to rest up. Turned out there might have been better places.'

Ugalde's eyes narrowed, as he finally broached the real issue behind his interrogation. 'And while you were *resting up*, did you just happen to cut the throat of one of my *sargentso*?'

Bannock regarded him impassively. 'Now why would I want to do a fool thing like that?'

'You tell me!' the *capitan* barked. His harsh tone caused the two uncomprehending *privados* beside him to jump. Instinctively fingering their muskets, they suddenly regarded the *Americano* with a degree of hostility.

It was then that Luis surprised both himself and Bannock, by coming up with an amazingly inventive response. 'It was the other *Americano* that killed your *sargento*. Señor Bannock tried to stop him.'

Now that *did* surprise the *capitan*. 'What other *Americano*?'

Luis shifted under the weight of his sleeping daughter, and gestured towards the still smouldering building. 'The one who is still in there, *patron*.'

Inside the church, Braxton had heard everything. 'Son of a bitch!' he muttered indignantly. He had no idea who this poxy *sargento* was that he was supposed to have killed, yet one thing was very apparent: 'The bastards are stitching me up!' But what to do about it?

A rapid glance around the smoking, and still intensely hot interior, provided no solace whatsoever. Tucked in his belt was a single Paterson Colt, which on closer inspection appeared to have one charged chamber remaining. That and a skinning knife in a sheath at his waist was the sum total of his weaponry. Not a lot to take on the Mexican army with! Yet he had to do something, and do it fast.

Then it came to him: the little bitch in the red dress. If he could get his hands on her, he would have something to barter with. Instinctively he reached for his knife. There was something about a razor-sharp blade at the throat that always seemed to concentrate people's thoughts – and besides, the Colt might be needed if some fool tried to crowd him. His right hand was still painful, but he could grip with it, which was all that mattered. From outside came the sound of heavy boots approaching. It was time to make his move!

Capitan Ugalde couldn't imagine that anyone might have survived such an inferno, but he was infinitely thorough in everything that he did. Motioning for the two *privados* to accompany him, he advanced on the church. None of the three had their weapons levelled, because the most any of them could have expected to find was a charred corpse.

The blackened apparition burst from the entrance, catching the *soldados* completely off guard. Before any of them could react, Braxton had barged past, desperately searching for a little figure in red. And for his dark intent, it couldn't have panned out better. There before him, recumbent in her father's lap, lay the picture of innocence that was Pepita.

Slightly beyond them, wide-eyed and startled, Bannock reached for a revolver in his belt, but his opponent just had the edge by a very narrow margin. Even as the hammer came back over a fresh percussion cap, Pepita's slim wrist was seized in an iron grip. As she awoke from a deep sleep, Luis attempted to grab her, but he couldn't match Braxton's animal strength. Stepping back, that other *Americano* swiftly altered his grip, so that his left arm was around her waist. Simultaneously his right hand, holding the knife, streaked up to her neck. With the vicious point suddenly probing her throat, he pivoted on his heels, executing a surprisingly graceful pirouette, so that no one would be in any doubt about whom he had hold of.

The little girl emitted a piercing scream, which initially served his purpose, but her captor soon tired of the noise. His left arm tightened around her, squeezing the air out of small lungs.

'Hush your mouth, missy, lest I cut you a new one,' he snarled, before addressing the adults around him. 'I won't take shit from no one. I don't know who I'm supposed to have kilt, and I don't give a damn. All I want is a horse, water, and free passage out of here. *Otherwise*, this little bitch is lost to you. Savvy?'

The two *privados* moved hesitantly towards him, until stilled by a sharp command from their officer. Luis, horrified by the abrupt turn of events, had scrambled to his feet, but could only look on helplessly as the unwavering blade threatened his beloved child. Bannock, by contrast, appeared unnaturally relaxed. Thrusting the still cocked Colt into his belt, he spread his arms wide in a gesture of contrition.

'In all my life, I've never heard of such a thing,' he

remarked softly. 'Holding a cutting tool on such an angel.'

Silas Braxton favoured him with a mirthless smile. 'Then you obviously don't get out enough, *Beaujolais* Bannock. 'Cause *I've* killed everything that walks or crawls, at one time or another.'

Ugalde apparently had no appetite for the death of a child. 'Put the knife down, and I promise you will go free,' he stated in his heavily accented English.

'You an' I both know that's a black lie,' Braxton spat back. 'So go to hell!'

Bannock recognized both the steely determination and total disregard for the life of an innocent. Then the knifepoint drew blood, and Pepita whimpered miserably.

'OK, that's enough,' he angrily acknowledged. 'Give him a horse, God damn it!'

'And water,' Braxton added gratuitously. He suddenly knew that he'd won, and he enjoyed the feeling.

Ugalde seemed prepared to accept the unsatisfactory outcome, but it came with a proviso. 'It cannot be either of our animals. The *teniente* and myself have to lead these men in another forced march tomorrow. *Coronel* Vallejo cannot cope without us, and he is not a man to cross.'

'So he can take one of the Comanche ponies, yeah?' Bannock persisted.

The *capitan* nodded silently. He disliked both of these *Americanos*, but not enough to risk having a child's blood on his hands. Luis, eager to do something, anything to save his daughter, rushed away to select an animal and a leather water container. He was back within moments.

'The bitch stays with me 'til I'm out of range of any muskets and such,' Braxton remarked.

'How do I know I can trust you?' Luis pleaded desperately.

'You don't,' was the uncompromising reply. With that, he whispered in his diminutive captive's ear. 'You hear me, my pretty? Take the reins from your pa, and keep a tight hold of them, or it'll go badly for you.' Braxton was no fool. He had no intention of releasing his hold on the girl.

Together, they shuffled awkwardly towards San Marcos's main entrance. *Teniente* Felipe glanced at his superior, and then reluctantly ordered their conscripts to make way.

Only once they were beyond the walls did Braxton remove the blade from Pepita's throat. Heaving her on to the pony's back, he then jumped up in front of her. His intention was obvious: he would use her as a human shield as they rode away.

'So long, Beaujolais,' he bellowed out, as he dug in his heels. That name again!

'What if he keeps her?' Luis wailed inconsolably, as the distance rapidly widened. 'He might even sell her to the Comanches!'

That grim thought had already occurred to Bannock. 'Where's my Hawken?' he demanded loudly. It came as no surprise when Tomas appeared, self-consciously holding the long gun.

'What a surprise,' Bannock remarked. 'This is

loaded, yeah?' As Tomas nodded firmly, he rapidly made for the nearest intact wall, checking the percussion cap as he did so. Braxton might have been beyond musket and pistol range, but a Hawken was something else altogether.

He deliberately mounted the steps at a steady pace. Breathlessness was the enemy of every sharpshooter. Cocking the rifle, he took careful aim at Braxton's right shoulder. The fugitive was using his left hand to hold Pepita in place behind him, which meant that she was mostly covering that side of his torso. With a distance of two hundred yards or so, his shot was a certainty. Gently, he squeezed one trigger, and then the next.

There was a pop, and then silence. Misfire!

Luis was outside, already mounted and ready to retrieve his beloved daughter. '*Señor*, why do you wait?'

Cursing, Bannock ignored him and rapidly considered his options. The cap had been sound. Ramming more powder and another ball down the barrel was pointless, and in any case risked blowing it up. That left one thing to try. Removing a nipple pick from his pocket, he probed the narrow channel leading down to the powder chamber at the rear of the barrel. And all the time Braxton was putting more distance between himself and San Marcos. It appeared that Luis had been correct. The *Americano* had no intention of releasing Pepita!

Praying that he had cleared any blockage, Bannock pressed another copper cap into position, and again levelled the rifle. This time it would be a long shot, in both senses of the word. Both windage and elevation had to be taken into account. Breathing steadily, he again drew a bead on Braxton's right shoulder. The margin for error was minute, but he didn't allow himself to dwell on the possible consequences. He just willed his way to the target and fired.

The welcome recoil jarred his shoulder, and Braxton jerked sharply before slumping forwards. His left hand must have suffered a spasm, because his prisoner suddenly tumbled clear. As a near frantic Luis kicked his pony into a gallop, Braxton continued on his way, making no attempt to turn around. Quite probably it took him every effort just to stay mounted.

Bannock smiled his satisfaction. It appeared as though the black-hearted scoundrel would live to fight another day – but he would certainly not forget this one.

CHAPTER THIRTEEN

After an uneasy night spent in the midst of many smouldering buildings, the *soldados* were lined up in two ranks, and about to be led out of the settlement by *Teniente* Felipe. In spite of the gruelling march ahead, all of them were glad to be leaving. Following the lighting of the massive charnel fire just beyond the walls, there had been a nauseating stench of death hanging over the place that would be a long time going.

Despite having certain reservations, *Capitan* Ugalde had come to the conclusion that there was little point in detaining the *Americano* known only as Bannock. There was no place to imprison him, and such a capable and dangerous man would just be a liability on a long journey. Perhaps more pertinently, there was also a complete lack of hard evidence against him. Yet he felt it only proper to offer some counsel.

'Take my advice, *señor*. Leave San Marcos, and leave Mexico . . . while you can.' As he stared intently at the man before him, the *capitan*'s expression was deadly serious. 'There is nothing here for you, and I believe with all my heart that it cannot be long before our two countries are at war.'

Bannock favoured him with a genuine smile. Thankfully this particular officer was at least reasonable. He knew for a fact that many weren't. He was mightily relieved that the soldiers were leaving without him, and he had indeed had a bellyful of Mexico.

'Don't fret yourself, captain. I've had my fill of Sonora, and will definitely be moving on. Oh, and thank you.' With that, he flipped him a casual salute, and then gratefully moved away to join Luis and his daughter. The sooner the infantry were gone, the better. He had seen the looks some of them had given him. It was obvious that not all of them believed him innocent of Montoya's killing. Whether he'd been a popular non-com or not, didn't come into it: the *sargento* had been one of them, and that was enough.

'Why don't you stay here with us for a while?' Luis enquired with obvious sincerity. Pepita clung to him, as she had since returning with him to the settlement the previous day. Her face had been smeared with some of Braxton's blood, but otherwise she was unharmed ... physically at least. 'After all that has happened,' he continued. 'You are most welcome. I . . . we owe you a debt that we can never repay!'

For a fleeting moment, Bannock had a stark vision of the girl with the red bonnet, but then mercifully it cleared. 'You don't owe me anything. Either of you,' he replied, adding cryptically, 'I was making amends.'

'But will you stay?'

The *Americano* smiled, but shook his head. 'I reckon

159

with all my heart that it cannot be long before our two countries are at war.'

Bannock favoured him with a genuine smile. Thankfully this particular officer was at least reasonable. He knew for a fact that many weren't. He was mightily relieved that the soldiers were leaving without him, and he had indeed had a bellyful of Mexico.

'Don't fret yourself, captain. I've had my fill of Sonora, and will definitely be moving on. Oh, and thank you.' With that, he flipped him a casual salute, and then gratefully moved away to join Luis and his daughter. The sooner the infantry were gone, the better. He had seen the looks some of them had given him. It was obvious that not all of them believed him innocent of Montoya's killing. Whether he'd been a popular non-com or not, didn't come into it: the *sargento* had been one of them, and that was enough.

'Why don't you stay here with us for a while?' Luis enquired with obvious sincerity. Pepita clung to him, as she had since returning with him to the settlement the previous day. Her face had been smeared with some of Braxton's blood, but otherwise she was unharmed ... physically at least. 'After all that has happened,' he continued. 'You are most welcome. I . . . we owe you a debt that we can never repay!'

For a fleeting moment, Bannock had a stark vision of the girl with the red bonnet, but then mercifully it cleared. 'You don't owe me anything. Either of you,' he replied, adding cryptically, 'I was making amends.'

'But will you stay?'

The *Americano* smiled, but shook his head. 'I reckon

not.' Gesturing towards the now departing soldiers, he added, 'The captain was right. There is nothing for me here. I sure ain't no farmer.'

Pepita stared up at him, her eyes like great pools. 'But where will you go?'

Bannock beamed down at her and winked, before returning his attention to her father. 'Thought I'd drift on over to Texas. Lot of demand there for a man with my skills. And who knows, I might just bump into Silas Braxton again. We never quite seem to finish it.'

There were so many questions that Luis could have asked him about that relationship, but he decided that it was probably better to hold his peace. Then one just kind of slipped out. 'Why did he call you Beau ... Beaujolais? What is it? What does it mean?'

Bannock's eyes momentarily grew cold, before he suddenly grunted and laughed. 'It's my given name, is what it is. My ma and pa must have sure had a strange sense of humour. Or mayhap they did it to toughen me up. Knowing that I'd have to fight plenty of folks over it. And I guess it worked, 'cause I'm still alive. But now, when anyone asks my name, I tell 'em "Bannock". Just "Bannock".'

'Well then, that's just how we'll remember you,' Luis commented, extending his right hand. 'Or possibly as the "Magnificent One". Wouldn't you like that?'

'Hah,' snorted the other man, as he gladly accepted the warm handshake. 'That does kind of have a nice sound to it!'